THE STARLIGHT CLUB 14

THE SICILIAN CAPER

BY
JOE CORSO

The Starlight Club 14: The Sicilian Caper, Joe Corso
Copyright 2022 by Joe Corso
Published by
Black Horse Publishing
Cover Art by Marina Shipova
Editing by BZHercules

Black Horse Publishing
www.blackhorsepublishing.com

This novel is a work of fiction. Names, characters, places and incidents are either the product of the author's imagination, or, if real, used fictitiously. No part of this book may be reproduced or transmitted in any form or by any electronic or mechanical means, including photocopying, recording, or by any information storage and retrieval system, without the express written permission of the author or publisher, except where permitted by law.

ALL RIGHTS RESERVED.

"The lion cannot protect himself from traps, and the fox cannot defend himself from wolves. One must therefore be a fox to recognize traps, and a lion to frighten wolves."

Niccolò Machiavelli, <u>The Prince</u>

TABLE OF CONTENTS

PROLOGUE 1
CHAPTER 1 3
CHAPTER 2 10
CHAPTER 3 17
CHAPTER 4 21
CHAPTER 5 31
CHAPTER 6 35
CHAPTER 7 41
CHAPTER 8 49
CHAPTER 9 61
CHAPTER 10 73
CHAPTER 11 79
CHAPTER 12 85
CHAPTER 13 91
CHAPTER 14 100
CHAPTER 15 119
CHAPTER 16 124
CHAPTER 17 137
CHAPTER 18 144
CHAPTER 19 153
CHAPTER 20 163
CHAPTER 21 173
EPILOGUE 180
AUTHOR'S NOTES 181

The Sicilian Caper

PROLOGUE

Present, Darien, Connecticut

Bobby was in the new room his daughter Lynn and her husband Ted had built for him, watching a Mets game. The room extended into the main house but was separated from it because, like now, her father enjoyed smoking a good cigar.

Bobby knew his daughter loved to listen to the stories he told her about the famous Starlight Club, so he visited his remaining friends who still lived in Corona. If you traveled back 50 years, you would have seen them in the Starlight Club, because they were a part of Red's crew and usually were at the bar sipping a drink or nursing a beer.

Most of Red's men who lived in Corona were gone now, but there were still a few old timers who remained. They had never moved from the old neighborhood, and were glad to meet with Bobby for breakfast or lunch. They still enjoyed a cappuccino made the old way sweetened with sambuca or anisette, and while they reminisced about the old days, Bobby quietly memorized the stories that were told to him. The results of his endeavors to collect and memorize various stories about the old Starlight Club, Red, Tarzan, Trenchie, Pissclam, and the rest of the men who were a part of Red's mob pleased him. Red and all of his men were part of the street and the streets gave you an education not learned in the higher courts of learning. Bobby now filed away several interesting stories gleaned from his meetings with the thinning herd of elderly gangsters. The one redeeming factor was the old timers loved to talk about the old days, when Red was running the mob, and the way it used to be at the old Starlight Club.

Lynn opened the door and walked in holding a tray with a

pot of the coffee and two biscotti. She knew her father enjoyed the combination of coffee and the few sweets she always brought with his coffee. "Mind if I join you, Dad?"

"Now when did I ever mind you joining me? In fact, now is a good time to join me because I have another tale to tell you about Red and the Starlight Club. But this tale begins before the Starlight Club was what it was at the height of its fame."

"I'm looking forward to hearing this story, Dad." She looked at the TV and smiled. "I guess this is as good a time as any." She pointed to the TV. "The Mets game just ended, so you can tell me the story without our being interrupted," Lynn said, smiling with the expectation of the story her father would tell her.

"Pissclam and a few of the boys shared this story with me over coffee last week, and it touches on Red's early years prior to his joining his uncle Yip's criminal organization."

CHAPTER 1

1961 Queens, The Starlight Club

It was early Monday morning when Joey Boy walked into the Starlight Club. He spotted Red sitting at his favorite table by the window near his office. He walked to the table. "Mind if I join you, Red?"

Red put aside the sports section of the *Daily News* he was reading and answered Joey Boy. "Not at all. Have a seat and join me. Do you want a cup of coffee?"

Joey Boy smiled. "I haven't had coffee yet this morning, Red, but a cup of coffee would hit the spot right now." Red poured a cup of the thick Italian espresso coffee and handed it to Joey Boy. "Do you want sambuca to sweeten it, or would you prefer sugar?"

"It's a little early, but I'll take a little sambuca."

Red handed him the bottle. "Take what you want and then tell me why you're here."

Joey Boy smiled as he poured a healthy shot of the sweet, anisette-flavored Italian liquor into his coffee and took a sip of his coffee before answering Red. "Do I have to have to want anything to enjoy a cup of coffee with my boss?"

Red put his cup down, and he gave Joey Boy a thin smile. "Cut the shit, Joey. No one comes here at nine in the morning just to bullshit with his boss. Now I'll ask you again... what do you want."

"I want nothing, Red, just maybe a little information. I was at Ziggy's last night and we got to talking about the old days, and he told me you, him, and Trenchie grew up together in this neighborhood, and you shared some hard times together."

"What else did Ziggy say?" Red said with a touch of anger

in his voice. He didn't like anyone telling tales about him to anyone, even a friend. "Go ahead. What else did Ziggy tell you about us?"

"He told me about how two scumbags killed your father in a restaurant when you were just a kid. He told me you and Trenchie never found the guy who pulled the trigger."

What else did Ziggy tell you?"

"Nothing, that's just it. He wouldn't elaborate on what happened other than to mention that they shot your father and killed him in a restaurant. I was hoping you would fill me in. I mean, the story was interesting and I have to be honest. I really wanted to know more about the old days and what you and Trenchie did when you were kids. I believe that happened before they made you, and before you owned the Starlight Club, right?"

Red didn't answer right away, and Joey Boy thought he wouldn't say anything more, but he did. "They killed my father when I was just a kid. It was before my initiation, and before I bought the King's Row bar and grill, before it became the Starlight Club." Red checked his watch. It was still early. "Pissclam, bring us another pot of espresso coffee." Red pulled a cigar from his leather cigar wallet. He offered Joey a cigar, which he refused. Red lit his cigar and sat back in his chair and waited for Pissclam to bring the coffeepot to the table. "I'm in a generous mood, Joey Boy, so I'll tell you a story. We're going back to 1945, before my uncle Yip considered bringing me into his organization."

1945, Queens, New York. The Corona Gentlemen's Club

There weren't many things that Yip loved, but his nephew Red was the one exception. Yip loved Red like he was his own son. He practically raised Red after Enzo Batto, a low level zit brought over from Sicily, killed Red's father. Vito Genovese brought Batto here to whack the president of a food chain. The man refused to pay protection to Don Vito. Vito gave the contract to two independent hit men, Enzo Batto and Willie Largi. But Enzo, with Willie as back-up, killed the wrong man in the sanctioned hit. They mistakenly killed Rocco, Red's father. When Enzo discovered his mistake, rather than face Don Vito's wrath, he packed a suitcase, took the cash he had stashed in his house, his passport, and then he flew back to Sicily where he hoped he would be safe from Vito's reach, and he lay low hiding in a cave high in the mountains he was familiar with that towered over the town he grew up in, Since Red's father was just a hardworking construction worker and wasn't a member of a mob, no one but Red, who was just a fourteen-year-old kid when they killed his father, swore to avenge his father's murder. He vowed to find Enzo Batto and Willie, and when he found them, he'd kill them.

1951

Yip studied his nephew, wondering if he was doing the right thing bringing him into his organization and giving him the job a few of the other men thought should be theirs. He thought there would be grumbling among the men, but he knew his nephew Red was a whiz with numbers, and besides, his most important consideration for giving him the job was that he knew beyond a doubt that he could trust Red. So with the thought that Red was his blood and that Yip instinctively knew he could trust his young nephew, he made his decision.

"Have a seat, Red," Yip said, pointing to the chair in front of his desk. When Red sat facing Yip, Yip continued. "I've been running this mob since before you were born, Red, and even though you balked when I insisted you attend college, you did what I asked you to do even though you didn't want to go. You didn't even know my motives for insisting you attend college. I had my reasons for wanting you to get an education. You see... I have plans for you. I decided that after you graduated college, I'd bring you into my organization. You'll start at the bottom, but when I retire... if guys like us can ever retire, I'd like you to be sitting in my seat, but before that happens, you'll have to show me you can run this organization. You'll start learning the numbers racket, and when you know it like the back of your hand, I'll have you run the operation. If you do well, and I'm confident you will," Yip explained, "you'll learn my loan-sharking operation, and from there, you'll learn Off Track Betting. Little by little, you'll learn every aspect of this operation, so when the day comes when you take over my rackets, you'll know everything there is to know about running our operation. You're good with numbers, so I'm confident you'll have no trouble learning every aspect of this business. When you start, you'll be in charge of several old timers, guys who started with me. It may disappoint them that you got the job instead of them, but they'll get over it. They're good men and they'll work hard for you, and they'll be loyal to you after you prove yourself to them. There may be some resentment among some of the old timers, since I'll have jumped you over them to get this job. But don't let that bother you, because like I said, they'll get over it. They may resent you not only because you're the new guy in charge, but because you haven't made your bones yet."

Yip lowered his voice and leaned closer to his nephew. "This is all new to you, Red, but you'll have to develop a sixth sense when dealing with the wiseguys. You'll learn to develop a sense of what the streets are telling you. Take a lesson from the old mountain men back in the early 1800s who developed a sixth sense when sensing danger from wild animals or Indians, or white men looking to kill them in their sleep, and take what was theirs. It was all automatic to the old mountain men. They just knew when danger was close without knowing how they knew it. They just sensed it. Wait and see. You'll learn how to sense danger without knowing how you did it. You must condition yourself to be aware of your surroundings at all times, just like those old mountain men did. We're in a dangerous business, Red. Other families want what we've built, and if we show weakness or if we don't pay attention to our business, our competitors will take what we've built from us.

"Then there is the federal and local law that's always looking to make their reputation by taking us down. You'll have to learn how to prevent that from happening. Trust no one. Trust only those who have passed your test. You'll know what the test is and when they've passed it, and then you will know you can trust that person." Yip had more to teach his nephew, but that could wait. He opened his humidor, pulled out a Cuban cigar, lit it, and leaned back in his chair. "Report here tomorrow morning. You'll start learning the numbers business from Sammy the Jew. He's been with me from the start and he's the best numbers man in the business, so listen to him and learn."

"Why is Sammy stepping down, Yip?"

"The doctors told him he has a lung condition, and they advised him to go west to Arizona or New Mexico for his health. Said the air out west was good for his lungs. I'm sending him to a contact of mine. While he's there, my contact will take him to see a lung specialist the doctors referred him to. He'll set him up with a place to stay and he'll hire someone to take care of him. I'll pick up the expenses. Shiv will make sure he lacks for nothing, and I'll see that Sammy has an income."

"That's big of you, Yip."

"It's not big, and it's not nice. It's good business, Red. I hate to lose him, but I take care of my men, unlike that cheap bastard Profaci who charges his men a ten percent vig. Tells them their money goes into an account for the families of his men who have to spend time in jail, but he keeps the money for himself. I don't do that. This is a dangerous racket we're in, so because of that, I take care of my men, and if they serve jail time, I take care of their family while they're away. I'm concerned about Sammy's health, but I'll do my best to ensure while he's out west, he gets the best health care possible. But." Yip said, pointing his cigar at Red, "you better listen to the Jew, and learn the business from the best, because I'm depending on you. In case you're wondering what your salary will be, I'll pay you $500.00 a week to start, plus ten percent of all the back due money you collect. Some customers decide they don't intend to pay us the money they owe us even though they have it, and other times they have the money, but they refuse to pay us for a month or two." Yip gave Red a dark look, which caused Red to shudder. "The people that owe us money must pay us the money they owe us, plus the interest that accrued on their loan. They always pay us. They know the penalty of not paying us when they borrowed the money. Remember, there is no excuse for not paying us." Yips saw the expression on his nephew's face and his look darkened. "I know what you're thinking," Yip said. "You're wondering what to do if a customer doesn't pay…

right?"

Red wanted to say something, but instead he gave a slight nod and listened to what Yip told him. "If they don't pay on their due date, the interest on their loan increases, along with a threat of what'll happen if they miss another payment. Sammy will explain all of this to you."

"What will I do if they miss a second payment, Yip?"

"You won't have to get your hands dirty attempting to collect our money. Sammy has a couple of enforcers working for him. They're good at their job, so put your mind at ease because you can make book they'll collect the monies owed us."

Red felt better when his uncle told him about the two enforcers, and he visibly relaxed while giving his uncle a questioning look. "Do the enforcers have names?" he asked.

"Yes. Your enforcers are Frankie Dead Eyes and Tommy the Wop, and they are two effective enforcers. They are not gentle, understanding men, so use them with caution. Use them when you have no other choice, because they'll get results… but at a price." Red wanted to question Yip, but again he held back, thinking better of it. Yip took a drag on his Cuban cigar and then he blew out a plume of blue smoke that clung to the ceiling. When Red didn't have any further questions, Yip stood and embraced his nephew.

"That's all for now, Red. Report to Sammy the Jew tomorrow at 10 am. He'll be waiting for you." Red stood to leave, but his uncle gently grabbed his arm to stop him. "Red, one more thing you should know before you leave. I trust my men, but I trust you more. Don't forget that and don't let me down."

"I won't, Uncle Yip."

"And don't call me Uncle Yip in front of the men. I don't want the guys thinking you got the job because of nepotism."

"I won't unc… I mean Yip."

"Good, now get out of here. See me tomorrow, after your meeting with Sammy." Red hesitated before leaving, which Yip observed."You have a question, Red?"

"No, Yip. I just wanted to clarify a misunderstanding you and the boys have about me."

The Sicilian Caper

Yip raised an eyebrow. "And what exactly is the misunderstanding you think we have about you?"

"You said I haven't made my bones yet, which is not true. I have made my bones."

Yip placed his elbows on his desk and leaned closer to his nephew. This news surprised him and he wanted an explanation. "Go ahead, I'm listening…"

CHAPTER 2

1945

Red went to his father's room and opened the hidden compartment in the closet, and he found his father's gun, and a box of 38-caliber ammunition. He loaded the Colt 38 police special, and he shoved the gun under his belt. He and his friend Trenchie took the El and got off the train at the Jackson Heights exit. They walked down the stairs to the bar under the El that Enzo hung out at in. It was dusk when they left the train, so they waited a little while for darkness to fall. He didn't want to go in there blasting, because he was a kid, and the men there would remember him. Instead, he opened the door and quickly scanned the room, looking for Enzo. Red noticed a customer heading toward him. At first, he thought the man would ask him what he was doing there, but the man walked by him and, as he was about to walk out the door, Red stopped him.

"Excuse me, but I'm looking for Enzo. Is he here?"

The man looked Red up and down suspiciously, and then seeing he was just a kid, he answered him. "Enzo was here, but he didn't stay long. He left about an hour ago, but his buddy Willie is still here. That's him at that table near the wall." It disappointed Red that he missed Enzo, but there was still Willie, and now that he saw that smug little bastard sitting at the table, he'd never forget him.

The two boys walked across the street to the malt shop and waited in front of it for Willie to leave the club. Red wanted to walk into the club and shoot the son of a bitch, and the hell with any pain-in-the-ass witnesses, but Trenchie convinced him it was better to wait until Willie left the club, and kill him when there were no witnesses that could point to the two kids as the shooters. A half hour later, the door opened and Willie walked

The Sicilian Caper

out, and as he crossed the street, he noticed two kids walking toward him. One kid appeared to be over six feet tall. The other kid was shorter, but they didn't appear to be a threat. Besides, he was a tough guy, and they were only kids, and he could handle them. The kids walked past Willie without looking at him, but when he passed, they turned around without Willie aware they were now following him. They waited for the right moment before acting, and they got that moment when Enzo approached an empty lot and he felt the press of iron on his back... and then he felt fear.

As they walked, Red said in a low voice so only Willie and Trenchie could hear. "You bag of shit... killed my father, and now I'm going to kill you, you fucking worthless prick, and when your back-shooting rat bastard friend Enzo returns, I'll be waiting for him, and when I see him, I'll kill him too," Red said darkly.

Willie knew the kid meant business, and he tried to bluff his way out of this dire situation. "Look, I'm not the guy you think I am. I didn't kill anyone. I don't even know the name of the guy you say I killed."

"The guy you two sons-of-bitches shot in the chest and killed was my father. You shot him like he was a rabid dog. His name was Rocco Fortunato. Now you know his name." Red pointed his gun at Willie's left shoulder and pulled the trigger. The bullet tore through Willie's shoulder, ripping bone and flesh out through the exit hole. A blossom of a pink mist of bone, tissue, and blood spewed like a halo around Willie as it punched through the exit wound, causing him to stumble, almost losing his footing. Willie was paste white as he grabbed his shoulder. It surprised him when he turned to see a kid pointing a gun at him. "Wait a minute, kid." Willie gasped for breath as he tried to clear his head and control the pain. "There's no need to shoot me. We can settle this with no further violence." Trenchie had heard enough of this punk's bullshit and he punched him with his ham-sized right hand hard on his chin, breaking the guy's jaw, causing him to spit out two teeth from his broken jaw as if they were chicklets. Then, without warning, Red shot him again, this time in his right shoulder, causing Willie to cry out again in pain. "Look at the tough guy crying," Trenchie said. "Look, Red, kill this prick and let's go home before someone hears the gunshots and calls the cops."

Willie tried raising his arm but it wouldn't work, so he tried to buy his way out of the dilemma he found himself in. "I just got paid, kid. You can have it all, but don't kill me. Please, I have a family, take the money... Please." Willie struggled to reach into his jacket pocket and with difficulty he pulled out an envelope. "Here, take it. It's all I have, but it's a lot of money."

"This the money you got for killing my father?" Red asked.

"Yes, er... no, er ... well, not exactly. It was an accident. We didn't mean to kill your father. It was mistaken identity. We thought he was someone else."

"Take the envelope, Trenchie." Trenchie reached over and took the envelope and put it in his pocket without checking what was in it. The guy was a dead man walking, and Trenchie knew it. "We done here?" Trenchie asked Red impatiently.

"Yeah, we're done here." Red pulled the trigger one last time and shot Willie in the head, leaving a gaping hole where the back of his head used to be. "Come on... let's get out of here." Red walked away, but Trenchie searched Willie's pockets before following Red, and he took what Willie had on him without bothering to check the items. He'd look the items over when they were alone.

"Where do you want to go, Red?" Trenchie asked.

"Let's go to Sal's poolroom. We can check out what this bum had on him there."

They found a dark corner table in the poolroom where they'd have a modicum of privacy. They took seats, and Trenchie, in the comforting darkness, laid some car keys, a money clip containing $230.00, and some change. Then he took the envelope he had placed in his pocket and laid that on the table.

"Open the envelope, Trenchie, but don't put it on the table. Lay it on the chair beside me, so no one but us can see it. Let's see how much money is in it. I hope he wasn't bullshitting us."

"Nah," Trenchie said. "The guy was trying to buy his life. He wouldn't bullshit us."

"Yeah, you're probably right, so open the envelope. I'm curious to see how much is in it." Trenchie counted out ten thousand dollars. "Not much money for taking someone's life," he whispered to himself, but loud enough for Trenchie to hear.

"You're right, it's not much money to take someone's life." Trenchie noticed the look of grief on his friend's face. "I'm sorry for your loss, Red."

"Thanks, Trenchie. I'm glad you were with me today. I don't know if I could have done what I did without you."

Trenchie laughed. "What do you mean you couldn't do it without me? You whacked the guy, and that's a fact. You had to do it, and you know you would have done it with or without me, so I don't want to hear any more about what you did today."

Red smiled, never thinking that there would be many more similar occurrences and discussions with his friend Trenchie in the years to come.

* * *

Pissclam knocked on Red's door. "Red, can I leave early? I feel like shit. Excuse me... I gotta use the head." Pissclam ran to the men's room. Fifteen minutes later, he sat in a chair in Red's office.

"Feel better, Pissclam?"

"I still feel like shit, but after that porcelain peeler I just took, I feel a little better. If it's all right with you, boss, I'd like to leave early. I'm so tired, my asshole just slid down around my ankles."

Red held back from laughing and Trenchie's lips separated into a thin smile. "Sure, go home. Tomorrow, if you don't feel better, call me and let me know how you feel. If you still feel lousy, stay home."

Pissclam shook his head. "Don't worry, boss, I'll be in tomorrow no matter how I feel," Pissclam said loud enough for Red to hear as he left the bar through the front door.

The side door opened and Jeannie Leg-and-a-half walked in. Jeannie had polio when she was just a kid. She survived it, but it left her with a deformed, shrunken leg, which caused her to shuffle, and she walked with a noticeable limp. Growing up in a big city, the kids could sometimes be cruel. They began calling her Jeannie Leg-and-a-half, and the nickname stuck.

Jeannie appeared to be in her late teens or early twenties. She stood 5 '4" tall, blond hair, fair skin with freckles on her cream-colored face. But even with her handicap, the neighborhood women were envious of her figure. Red knew that Jeannie never thought of herself as being pretty, or having a splendid figure. Her shriveled leg, she thought, made her less of a woman, and less desirable to men, and maybe that was why she never had an actual boyfriend. Sure, boys dated her once in a while, but always with the thought that because of her leg, she'd be an easy lay. They soon found they were wrong. Jeannie was a proud young lady who had the respect of the neighborhood men who knew her. One of those men was Big Red Fortunato. Red enjoyed talking to her, and when she came home late sometimes, he would have one of his men walk her home. She lived in the last house on Forty-second Avenue at the end of the block opposite the entrance to the Grand Central Parkway. It was dark there at night, and even though this was a relatively safe neighborhood, Red felt better knowing one of his men would make sure she arrived safely home.

"What brings you in here at this time of night, Jeannie?"

"I had a dream about you last night, Red, and I have to tell you about it."

That got Red's attention. Very few people knew Jeannie had the gift of precognition. Jeanie didn't consider herself a psychic, but her mother, and her mother's mother before her, had the gift, which was passed down from mother to daughter to her. She didn't like it; she didn't want it, but she had it. Her gift came to her mostly in her dreams, but in rare instances, her gift appeared to her in a flash of insight, but it was a rare occurrence.

"Come into my office, Jeanne. Do you want a cup of coffee, or perhaps a drink?"

"Thank you, Red. Coffee would be nice."

Red poured her a cup of the strong espresso coffee and sweetened it with a shot of the Italian licorice-flavored anisette. "Biscotti, Jeannie?"

"No, Red, just coffee is fine." She opened her pocketbook and removed a few small sheets of paper with writing on them. "I wrote some notes while the dream was still fresh in my mind." She looked up at him with fear in her beautiful but frightened blue eyes. "I'm sorry, Red, but late one night when no one is here, something bad will happen to this place. It appeared in my dream that it would occur soon."

Red knew from experience to take this perceptive young woman's dream seriously. In the past, events happened as her dreams predicted.

"There is someone who hates you. He will return and will seek revenge, first by destroying what you love and then he will attempt to kill you." She looked up at him again, this time with tears glistening in her pretty blue eyes. "Be careful, Red."

Red tensed himself before asking her, "Will he hurt, or kill me?"

"No, Red." He visibly relaxed when he heard those words. "Not this time, Red, but when they destroy your famous second bar, you will be seriously injured."

"Will they kill me?"

"No. You will hover between life and death for a while, but you will survive." Red had several questions that needed answers. "The first time they destroy my bar, who are the people responsible?"

"One person, with the help of others, will destroy this place, and it will happen soon."

"And the second time?" Red asked.

"The government will destroy the famous club, but it will occur in the future."

"Did your dream reveal the name of the person who will destroy my club?"

"No, but he is an old enemy, someone you used to know." Jeannie looked up with sad eyes. "Do you know the man in my dream, Red? The man is evil. Be careful. He hates you, and he won't rest until you're dead."

Red smiled grimly. "Thank you for the warning, Jeannie. I appreciate it, but don't worry about me. I'll be on guard now that you've warned me about the potential danger."

Jeannie's eyes became slits, and she hissed, "It's not potential danger, Red, it's real danger. Don't you understand, my dreams never lie. Until the threat is over, you must be on your guard at all times. Promise me you'll take my warning seriously. Please, Red, promise me you'll be careful."

Red put both his arms on Jeannie's shoulders and he looked into her eyes. "Have you ever known me not to listen to your advice, Jeannie? Now that you've warned me, I will be extra cautious. I think I know the man in your dream. If that is the man, he killed my father, but he made a mistake by not killing me when he had the chance."

The Sicilian Caper

CHAPTER 3

Red and Trenchie had been comfortably running the numbers for over a year. He had brought in the one man, Trenchie, he knew he could trust above all others with him. He made his large friend his chief enforcer, placing him in charge of his two other enforcers. Trenchie was 6'5" and when he came to collect money from a customer that was late with their payment, they somehow found the money to pay him. The few that couldn't pay he gave a day to find the money, and knowing the consequences of not coming up with the money, in just about every case, they somehow found the money. The amount of late monies collected by Red through Trenchie's efforts impressed Yip. One payday, Red told Yip he'd like to split his ten percent with Trenchie because he felt Trenchie deserved it. Yip refused Red's request, but he surprised Trenchie by giving him five percent of all overdue monies he collected on top of the ten percent he gave to Red. Trenchie accepted the five percent, but as was his nature, he showed no emotion when Yip handed him his paycheck and he found it included an extra five percent garnered from all the overdue late money he collected.

On payday at the Corona Gentlemen's Club, Yip told Red to remain after everyone left.

"I'm impressed with the job you did with our numbers business. It's running smoother than ever and we're averaging a twenty percent increase in revenue. That's impressive, and because of the job you're doing with the numbers, I'm giving you the loan-sharking operation to work, and since I figure you'll do the same with loan-sharking, I'm giving you a raise. From now on, you'll earn a grand a week, and I'll finance the renovations for the bar you bought. Consider it a bonus for a job well done. Report to Gus at the Ridgewood warehouse. He's our loan-sharking guru. I'll call him and let him know that I put you in charge of loan-sharking. Remember that the numbers and loan-sharking rackets are two sides of the same coin. One goes with the other. I want you to combine the two into one racket. Can you do that for me?"

"Why not? Like you said. Those two rackets are two sides of the same coin, but if you agree, I'll take Trenchie and the two enforcers with me. I'll have Trenchie show them the proper way to get our customers to pay their debt, just like he does."

"Good, I like that," Yip said, happy with his nephew's performance. Without Red knowing it, Yip spread the word to his captains that Red had made his bones, explaining to them how he did it. As that bit of news circulated among Yip's crews, Red's stock shot way up. Now, whenever the men met with Red, they treated him as a man to respect.

A year passed, and Yip called Red to a meeting. Red knew he did a good job with the numbers, money lending, and loan-sharking, so he wasn't worried about his performance, but he wondered why his uncle called him to this meeting. When he entered Yip's office, no one was there but Yip. Then the door opened and Fat Charlie escorted Trenchie in. Fat Charlie was one of Yip's captains. As soon as he seated Trenchie, he left the room, closing the door behind him. Trenchie gave Red a questioning look, hoping for a silent answer, but Red, who was just as lost as Trenchie, shrugged his shoulders. Yip directed his gaze at Trenchie, and then at Red, and after a lengthy pause, he began speaking. "I suppose you're wondering why I summoned you to my office. Right?"

Both young men just nodded.

"Put your mind at ease, boys. You did nothing wrong, but I have a surprise for both of you. Trenchie didn't like surprises, and neither did Red, because surprises never boded well for them, but they kept their mouths shut and waited for the trap-door to open.

Yip laughed out loud. He was enjoying their discomfort. "Relax. I told you, you did nothing wrong. In fact, you two did such a good job. I know you'll like what I'm about to tell you. It's my little surprise."

The Sicilian Caper

Yip let the moment linger a little longer, and then he became serious. The two young men noticed the change in Yip when his eyes narrowed on Trenchie with a portentous look, and then his foreshadowing look shifted to Red. Then the suspense lifted when Yip smiled, showing a full set of white gleaming teeth. "Relax, guys. The books are open again, and because of the job you two have done with our numbers, moneylending, and our bookmaking, you've doubled our yearly revenues. Because of that, even though you're both a little young, I've recommended to the commission that the two of you and Ziggy take the oath on Saturday, and they approved it. We will make you three made men. Men of honor after your induction into our thing... or... La Cosa Nostra.

"Be in my office Saturday at 8 am, dressed to the nines, wearing your Sunday best. Dress like you were going to your wedding... understand?"

Both men nodded. "I didn't hear you!" Red said loudly with his both hands on his ears.

"I'll say it again in case you knuckleheads are hard of hearing. DO YOU UNDERSTAND?"

Both men understood the seriousness of the moment. "Yes, I understand," they said almost in harmony.

"Good!" Yip said, barely able to stifle the smile that threatened to surface on his tough, unforgiving face. "Get out of here now... I'll see you two Saturday morning... and don't be late." When his nephew and Trenchie left, Yip slumped deep in his plush chair, thinking of the finality of what he just did to his nephew. He thought his nephew was strong enough to handle the change in direction his life would take from that moment on, but on Saturday, his life would irrevocably change. He hoped for the better, but who could tell one's destiny. He didn't know, but one thing was for sure, his life would no longer be his. Red would pledge his life to this family until the day he died when the knife cut his finger and his blood dripped onto the contract, sealing the promise he made to the family. *Does Red understand what he's committed his life to?* he wondered. *Could he handle this alternative lifestyle?* Yip hoped so.

When Red left his uncle, he thought about what had just happened. After Saturday, he'd be a made man. He appreciated his uncle's philosophy. Sure, if he felt it necessary, Yip would kill a man, but only if it was necessary, and not plain murder. Yip was like the government who sentenced men to the death penalty, because they did something deemed by the courts as punishable by death. The person pulling the switch on the electric chair, or the person dropping a cyanide tablet that killed the man on death row strapped to the chair didn't get pleasure from killing the man, but it was his job and it was necessary. That was how Yip judged the man who broke the family's rules. He didn't take pleasure in ordering a man's death, but it was necessary. Red learned from that example and he hoped he'd never be in a position where he had to enforce that rule. He knew someday he'd rule his uncle's empire. He just hoped he could rule it with the wisdom his uncle did.

CHAPTER 4

1950

    Red and Trenchie took seats at a table near the bar, talking. "Have you thought of a name for your bar, Red?" Trenchie asked.

    "Don't laugh, but I've thought of a name. Just don't know if I'll use it. I'll have to think on it awhile." Red's reticence to tell Trenchie the name he was considering for his bar piqued his friend's interest, and he was like a hound dog on the scent. "You going to tell your good buddy the name you're thinking of using… or are you going to be selfish and keep it to yourself?" Trenchie asked sarcastically, but with a hint of a smile on his face.

    Red was unsure he'd use the name, thinking it was stupid, but he always trusted Trenchie's opinion, because he never held back, always telling it the way he saw it. So Red shared the name he was thinking of using with his friend. "I watched *Casablanca* on the television a few nights ago, and since the name of Bogart's joint was 'Rick's Place', I thought I'd name my joint 'Red's Place.' I was even thinking of decorating my bar like Rick's in Casablanca." Trenchie chuckled. "What's funny, Trenchie?"

    "If you named this joint Red's Place, you wouldn't need a decorator because this place looks just like Rick's without your renovating it."

    "You're not just saying that, are you?"

    "I'm not kidding, Red. I'm as serious as a heart attack. Save yourself a lot of bucks, and leave the place as it is, but add things that give the place that exotic Casablanca look, like those old-fashioned ceiling fans Rick had in his place. Hire someone who knows about these things and have them put the finishing touches on the place, and with their help, Red's Place will be set to open in no time."

Red smiled for the first time that day. "Trenchie, you're a genius. The answer to my dilemma was staring me in the face, but it took my buddy Trenchie to point it out to me."

Something about the name and look of his bar nagged at Red, but having no other ideas for his bar, he gained several original interior and exterior copies of the concept sketches for Casablanca from a contact of Yip's at Warner's. Red wasted no time in handing the drawings to his architect. He paid the man a substantial down payment to begin work on the changes to the exterior and interior of Red's Place to match the exact look of Humphrey Bogart's, Rick's Place, in Casablanca. It satisfied Red now that he knew they would work on both the interior and exterior, figuring by them working on both the inside and the outside, it would cut his new club's opening time in half.

Two weeks later, Red wore a hint of a smile as he studied the completed facade. His uncle Yip recommended a contractor and Red took his suggestion and used the man. Where the hell he found the contractor, Red didn't know. He shook his head, smiling. Because the damned contractor got it right, he thought. He held a picture of Casablanca's Rick's Cafe American, then he looked up at the completed entrance to his bar. The only difference between the name change. Casablanca's entrance said 'RICK'S AMERICAN CAFÉ' in neon script while his sign read 'RED'S AMERICAN CAFÉ.' Neon tubes crowned the name above and below, completing the signage. The architect duplicated the neon sign exactly the same way as it appeared in the movie. Red's gaze drifted down and he assessed the rest of the entrance's facade. And he appreciated the outside entrance they created for him. It was perfect, as if the contractor found the movie's original Ricks American Cafe entrance facade Warner's built to use in *Casablanca* locked away in an old forgotten warehouse and trucked it across the country to Queens, that was how good a job they did with the front of the building, he thought. Red had been conducting business from his office in the rear part of the building, but when they started renovating the interior, they asked him to leave until they completed it.

It was the longest two weeks he had ever waited for something. He didn't know how the interior looked now that they completed it, and he was eager to see it. The contractor in charge of the project, Artie, knew from his body language what was on his mind. "Go on in. Look around and let me know how you like it."

"Thanks. You read my mind, Artie. I'm eager to see how the renovations came out."

"I'll go in with you and answer questions you may have while you check out the modifications we made," Artie said.

They walked through the front door because Red wanted to see every part of the renovation, starting from the front door, then working their way to the back. Artie showed him all the changes they made, figuring if Red wanted to add or change any of the additions they could do it while his construction crew was still putting the finishing touches on the outside facade... but Red loved what Arty and his construction crew did to the place and he wouldn't have Artie change a thing, even though his construction crew were still there working on the place.

Artie left the front bar as it was, so it was basically unchanged, except they refinished the entire bar from top to bottom. They took the dark wood stain off, right down to the original wood, and then they re-stained the wood with a dark walnut stain. Then Arty had his men resurface the bar top with the same walnut stain they used on the sides. The following day, when the stain had dried, to protect the wood, they coated the bar top with an acrylic-based resin. Arty informed Red that he chose an acrylic resin because of its ease of use and because it wouldn't chip or break, and it had an extra benefit. It had a Class 1 Fire Rating, making the bar extremely safe. Red nodded and turned his attention to the floors and walls, which now had an old-fashioned look, which matched Bogart's club in Casablanca. They gutted the kitchen area and completely rebuilt the room to modern standards. Before entering his office, Artie stopped Red and said something to him. "I forgot to tell you I installed an item that wasn't in your original order. I hope you don't mind." That got Red's interest. "What the hell did you install that I didn't ask for, Arty?"

"It gets mighty hot in the summer, Red. If you want to cool off, you either go to the beach or you go to see a movie, right?"

"Right." Red said, seeing where this was going.

"I took the liberty of installing central air-conditioning in your place."

"What's this going to cost me, Arty?" Red said testily.

"One of my competitors closed up his shop. He called me and asked if I wanted to buy his inventory. I said I'd look at what he had, and if I liked it and the price was right, maybe I'd buy a few items. When I entered his warehouse, I thought I hit the lottery. He had equipment I needed, a lot of 2 x 4s and 2 x 6s, and plenty of tools... and guess what else he had?"

Red's eyes lit up. "A commercial air conditioner."

"Bingo," Arty said, laughing. "Not one, but two sets of central air conditioners. I said I'd buy every item from him if he threw in the A/Cs."

"Well, did he?" Red asked, curiosity getting the best of him.

"He said he couldn't do that, but he'd throw one A/C in if I took everything else. It so happened I could use all the items he was getting rid of, including the spare air conditioner."

"So what's the A/C going to cost me?" Red asked.

"Look, Red, the air conditioner didn't cost me anything, so I'll throw it in. But I expect to get a lot of meals gratis from you when the bar opens for business."

Red put his arm around Artie's shoulder, and as they walked to the door, he told him, "I intend to serve food here, so you'll never have to pay for a meal in this place, Artie, and that's carved in stone."

"Thanks, Red."

Seven am the following day, when Artie and his construction crew arrived at the site to begin work, it stunned them to find police tape wrapped around the building and the fire department busy placing their hoses back on their large red fire engines. They destroyed the wall facing the street, leaving a gaping hole where the wall used to be. The bar, office, and small dining room were in shambles.

Because of the noise the construction crew made in the early mornings, Red stayed in a temporary room in the Airport motel near LaGuardia Airport so he could get a good night's sleep.

The Sicilian Caper

Artie called the Airport motel and woke Red up. A half hour later, a groggy, furious Red arrived at his bar and saw what was left of his dream.. Artie, Ziggy, and a police officer watched Red pull his Caddy to the curb and park across the street from the bar. When he approached the damaged building, a cop held fragments of hand grenades in his hand. Red knew most of the police officers in the 110th, but he didn't recognize this officer. "Officer Brian O'Malley, the chief investigator in the 110th." O'Malley put his hand out and Red took it. "Sorry to have to meet under these circumstances, but our forensic team discovered hand grenade fragments, and it was obvious this was what caused the damage to the structure. The perps threw hand grenades through the windows and into the rooms, and then they got out of Dodge in a hurry. Grenades caused the damage, and luckily, they didn't damage the upper floor. It looks like your club will be lit by starlight, because until they can rewire the place, the only light you'll have is starlight from the heavens." The cop was talking, but what he just said lit a light in Red's mind, and he suddenly knew what had been nagging at his mind. It was the name and decor that had been troubling him. He liked the Casablanca theme, but that wasn't the result he envisioned. He wanted something memorable, something that would resonate with the peoples of the world, and now he knew what that was. Red smiled broadly, confusing the officer. O'Malley raised an eyebrow, and he gave Red a sidelong glance. "Did I just say something funny, Mr. Fortunato?"

"No, you didn't say something funny, but you said something important to me, and it's not Mr. Fortunato. It's Red to you."

"Oh? And what did I say that was important to you, Red?"

"When you told me the only light I'd have for a while is starlight, now that was important to me."

O'Malley narrowed his eyes and asked, "So what's important about that, and why is it important to you?"

"It means nothing to anyone but me," Red said. "Because Starlight's going to be the name of my new club. I'm naming it the Starlight Club."

Although that was important to Red, it wasn't to O'Malley.

"That's fine, Red, but the question remains... why did they

target your place?" The cop furrowed his brow and gave Red a long look before speaking. "Do you know anyone who could have done this?"

"No." Red said, shaking his head. "Why?"

"Because it looks to me that someone had a major hard-on for you. Are you sure you don't know anyone who had a gripe against you?"

"No, I don't," Red told the cop a second time. Then he paused and thought of Enzo. *Is he back in town? Could Enzo be behind this?* he asked himself. With that thought in the forefront of his mind, he swore he would find out if that snake Enzo was back, and if he was, could he have caused the damage to his bar?

"Excuse me, sir." O'Malley turned to one of his men. "We found grenade fragments in the kitchen area, but we got lucky because the explosion didn't damage the gas jets in the kitchen. If the grenades ruptured the gas lines, the entire block could have gone up in one hell of an explosion. Come with me and I'll show you what I mean." Red watched O'Malley disappear into the kitchen with the officer, and as he turned, he bumped into Ziggy. The two were close friends. Ziggy grew up with Red and Trenchie, and they had always remained close friends. "What are you doing here, Ziggy?"

"The explosion was on the local news, and I thought you might need some help. I came here for two reasons. The first is I came over to watch your back… just in case."

Red hadn't realized that the guys that did this could still be close by, and if that was true, then when the cops left, he could still be in danger. "I hadn't thought of that, Ziggy, but I'm glad you came, because now that you mention it, Trenchie hasn't been around and I could use someone to watch my back."

"Well, I have a suggestion for you, Red, if you care to hear it."

Red gave Ziggy a questioning look before answering, "Let's hear it, Ziggy."

"This bar isn't for you. I should have mentioned it sooner, but it just isn't big enough for what you have in mind, but there is a local club available that just went on the market, and it'd be perfect for you, and best of all, you can get it at the right price."

The Sicilian Caper

"Where is the bar located? Is it in Queens? If it's not, I'm not interested."

"It's the old King's Row bar and grill on 43rd Avenue."

Red's eyes lit up. "Yeah, I know the place. That's the place where back in the twenties a gunman walked in and shot and killed a guy sitting at a table by the window."

"That's the place." Ziggy said.

"If I wanted to buy that place, I still have a problem. I still have to do something with this place."

"You had insurance for this place, right?"

"Yeah… So?"

"Sell the place to me, and I'll pay you whatever the insurance doesn't cover. Since my crew works in this part of Queens, I must have a place to work out of and the location of this place is perfect for me. If you'll sell this place to me, I'll rebuild it and use it as my base of operations."

"Come on. Let's look at the old King's Row bar and grill. I already have a name for the place, so if I like it, maybe it'll do. Let's take a ride and see what it looks like."

Murray Goldman gave Red a walk through each room of the old bar and grill. The long bar was impressive. It was still in excellent shape and it reminded him of the old Longhorn bar in Tombstone when, as a kid, he visited many years ago with his uncle Yip. The kitchen was too small for what Red envisioned, but he said nothing. He could always expand it if necessary. Goldman showed them a storage room that Red knew would be his conference room. The cellar was ancient, and it looked as if it came out of the 1800s with gas pipes running at intervals along the length of the old cellar. It even had levers on the pipes to turn the gas on and off, which were still active. It surprised Red to see a fully functional bowling alley set up alongside the stairs leading into the cellar. Murray noticed Red staring at the bowling alley. "We built that for a bowling club that used to practice for tournaments, but when they left, they left the alley just the way you see it. Come on. I have one more thing to show you." Goldman led them back upstairs to the small office and Red waited for the one more thing Murray still had to show him. Red looked at his watch and then at Murray. "You said you had something else to show me, Murray. It's getting late, so let's see it before I leave."

"Sure. Follow me, Red. It's just beyond the kitchen." Red and Ziggy followed Murray to a shuttered wall. Murray pushed a button on the wall, and the shutters folded in on themselves as the wall opened. Red stared into darkness until Murray pressed the button, which turned on the lights, which illuminated the beautiful but tired-looking old ballroom from decades past. Murray explained they had hardly used the large hidden ballroom in the past forty years... "I use it once or twice a year for occasional weddings or bar mitzvah."

"Why don't you use it more often?" Red asked.

"We don't have a cabaret license to do that. When we use the old ballroom, we take an envelope to the captain of the 110th precinct and he looks the other way."

"What are you asking for the place, Murray?"

"Fifteen thousand buys the entire building."

"What if I gave you a check for twelve grand right now? Would we have a deal?"

Murray considered Red's offer, but he shook his head. "Make it thirteen thousand and give me a check right now and we'll have a deal, and that'll include the bar's inventory."

"Let's go into your office and we'll consummate the deal right now."

When Red handed Murray the check, he asked to be shown the apartments upstairs. There were three apartments and Red decided he'd live in the rear apartment because it had a rear porch with a fire escape near the alley behind the club. He'd save the two other apartments for guests.

When they went back downstairs, Murray handed Red the deed to the building, along with two sets of keys and a copy of the building's insurance. "You'll have to call your insurance agent and duplicate this policy or ask them to add the provisions you feel you need and take out the ones you don't want." After Murray left with his check stuffed tightly in his wallet, Red sold Ziggy the remnants of his wrecked bar. "Are you sure you want to do this, Ziggy?"

"I'm sure, Red. I have the dough to rebuild the place. I just want a place that will pay its keep and offer me a place to work out of. That bar will work out nicely for me and it'll be worth every cent I put into it."

"Okay," Red said. "As long as you're happy, then I'm happy." Red opened his attaché case and pulled out the deed to his destroyed building. "I'll write up a bill of sale for the agreed upon price and you can take it to your lawyer to re-write. Bring it to me after you see your lawyer and I'll sign it, so you can register it." After negotiating a fair price for the damaged building, Ziggy turned to leave, but Red stopped him. "One more thing, Ziggy. Find another construction crew because I'll need Artie here to renovate this place."

"No problem, Red. I have someone else I can use."

"Good," Red said as Ziggy turned and walked out through the front door. Red watched Ziggy get in his car, and when he drove away, Red called Artie and told him he bought a new club and he needed to see him as soon as possible. He gave him the address and told him to come as soon as he could. He'd be there waiting for him. Artie knew not to keep Red waiting, so he gave orders to his work supervisor to dismiss the men and instruct them to show up for work tomorrow morning at 7:30 am at the new address. "Do you have a pencil?" he asked, and then he gave him the address to the job-site to write down.

Artie and his work supervisor Jake Winters arrived at Red's new bar in Corona where an anxious Red waited for them. Red gave both men a yellow secretary's pad and a pencil. "Take notes while I show you the place and tell you what I want done to it." Then he gave them a tour of his new bar. He told them what he wanted the bar, the ceiling, and floor to look like, and then he led them to the kitchen. "This has to be expanded. I'd like the kitchen to be larger. I expect someday soon, I will overbook this place with customers trying to get dinner reservations." The two men thought the meeting was over, but Red motioned for them to follow him. He opened the folding wall leading into the ballroom and put the lights on. The size of the room impressed the two men, especially Artie. His eyes lit up. "Man... this room has great possibilities. What do you want me to do with the room?" he asked Red.

"Put new hardwood floors for people to dance on. I want a small stage and podium built. Install speakers, microphones, lights, and a ceiling that resembles the stars in the heavens.

Install indirect lighting throughout the room. Oh… and I'd like a special small nook for me and my guests built over there." he said, pointing to a nook that would practically hide him and his guests. "Next, I want you to take the storage room and build me a conference room, and last but not least, I want an impressive sign built for the Starlight Club."

"The Starlight Club? Is that what you're going to name this place?"

"That's right. It's the new name for this place. Bring me some artists' renderings to choose from. If I don't like what you bring me, I'll have you bring me more to look at. Understand?"

"I'll do that, Red. You know, I can remove the air conditioner I just installed in your bar and install it in this place. Do you want me to do that?"

"If it was anyone but Ziggy, I'd say do it, but he's buying a wrecked joint, so let's leave it the way it is."

Artie sighed. "I'm going to get hammered on this job, but since this place doesn't have air conditioning, I'll install the other air conditioner I have and we'll figure a way for you to pay me without the price killing you."

CHAPTER 5

It was early morning, and Red had to think. He couldn't think in a room crowded with Artie and his men banging on walls and tearing up floors. He went to the kitchen and made a pot of coffee. When it was ready, he poured himself a cup and carried it upstairs past his bedroom to the small back patio next to the fire escape. Red placed the coffee on the small wrought-iron table. The bedroom phone ringing interrupted him just as he was about to sit down. *What now?* A phone call this early was never a good sign, he thought. Red picked up the phone on the night table. It was Yip. "Put down whatever you're doing and get here as fast as you can. I have something important to tell you."

Red left his coffee on the coffee table, bolted down the stairs, and was out the door. In less than ten minutes, he was in Yip's office, seated at his desk opposite him. "What's wrong, Yip? You said you had something to tell me. What happened?" With bloodshot eyes, Yip leaned forward and rested his hands on his desk, and he gave his nephew a tired look. Red thought his uncle had aged ten years since yesterday. "What's wrong Yip?" he asked again.

Yip looked at his nephew through bloodshot eyes. He hesitated a moment before speaking, knowing he would hurt his nephew by what he had to tell him.

"They arrested Trenchie for manslaughter."

"What?" Red said, louder than he intended.

Yip then told Red about last night's attempt to kill him. "The rats wanted to take over my Queens rackets, and I stood in their way."

"Who was involved, Yip?"

"Big Head Strunzi was behind the attempted takeover. If it wasn't for Trenchie, I would be a dead man. Trenchie spotted two men sitting in the car across the street. Me and Trenchie walked through the backyards and made it up the street away from Big Head to where we could cross the street without being seen. When we got closer to his car, we hid in the shadows. While Trenchie covered me with his handgun, I got close to them without them spotting me, and then I shot both men, but there was a third guy across the street that I didn't see. He must have been casing my office. The point is... I didn't see him... but Trenchie did. Just as the guy was about to plug me, Trenchie yelled out a warning to me. The shooter swung around, and instead of shooting me, he shot Trenchie twice. While his attention shifted from me to Trenchie, I took advantage of it. His warning gave me the time I needed to shoot and kill the bastard. But Trenchie was down and I was afraid he might be dead. I ran to help him and when I got to him, he was still alive, but badly injured. I was about to get him to the car and rush him to the hospital when we heard the sirens. Trenchie pushed me away. 'Go... The cops... are coming. No sense... both of us getting caught. Get out of here,' Trenchie gasped, and then his eyes closed. I had hoped he just passed out and hadn't died. I guess we were lucky, because he's alive and in the hospital. I'm afraid he's going to be given a long sentence. I hope not. That's why I called Doc. Maybe he could reach out to a few of his contacts to see if they could help. Stick around, Red. I'm expecting him at any moment."

Doc walked in and sat down wearily and shook his head. "I tried, Yip, but no matter who I called and what I tried, nothing helped. In the end, with all of my contacts, the DA told me, with three dead bodies, Trenchie is looking at a minimum of ten years in the big 'Q,' San Quentin."

Red buried himself in work, trying to dismiss the pain he felt about Trenchie being away. Yip watched the way his nephew handled the many assignments he kept giving him, and with nary a complaint from his nephew. Red thrived on the challenges he handed him. Red was ready. He learned the many facets of his illicit rackets. He refined and improved them, which resulted in a major increase in a profitable revenue flow.

The Sicilian Caper

Since Red was now a made man, with smooth running rackets, it allotted him more time to spend at his bar. He even conducted his mob business from his office near the ballroom. Plus, Yip gave him a small monthly percentage of the millions generated from his rackets, with most of the money brought in by his crews going to Yip.

As the months and years passed, whenever Yip called his captains to a meeting, Red watched and learned how Yip ran the meeting, and how he ran his organization. Yip was an excellent leader of men. If they were loyal and were good earners and they followed orders, then those men rose in the ranks, earned more, and he gave them greater responsibilities. The men knew some bosses of other crime families kept most of the money for themselves, and shared none of the profits with their men. In contrast, Yip's men were grateful to be a part of his organization.

Yip was a student of history, especially the Roman Legions. When the legions defeated their enemy and when they took control of their towns, in almost every instance, they permitted the legionaries to loot the town, rape the women, and the residents taken to be sold as slaves in Rome's slave market. Every Legionnaire knew selling slaves earned them the real money.

Most of the money Yip received from the rackets went straight into his pockets, but he placed a percentage of the money in a special fund to be used to support the families of men sent to prison, plus he made sure his men received a generous percentage. He gave bonuses to the crews that had an exceptional money-earning year. The money came from rackets Yip considered harmless. His loan-sharking business supplied a need for men or women that couldn't get a loan from banks. Sure, his interest was higher than a bank, but the money served a need to the person who borrowed it. The same rule applied to his bookmaking operation and numbers racket. A person who couldn't get to the track to bet on a horse could take advantage of Yip's bookmakers and make their bets locally without having to travel miles to a track to place their bets. His truck hijackings were always without blood flowing. Yip made a fortune from his illicit rackets. He was making so much money, not dealing with drugs and women, that his crews knew never to venture into the dark waters of drugs and prostitution. "Stay away from the white powder. If I catch any of you dealing in the white powder, I promise you I will kill the man myself. The same goes for women. If I hear any crew is putting women to work on the streets, I will treat that man or that crew exactly as if he were selling drugs. I know there's a ton of money selling drugs and women, but we're doing all right sticking to what we do best. The law mostly turns a blind eye to what we do, because we're not harming anyone and we're offering our people a harmless service. But the moment we deal in drugs and women, they'll be on us like stink on shit."

The government sentenced many men to the death penalty because they did something deemed by the courts as punishable by death. The person pulling the switch on the electric chair or the person dropping a cyanide tablet and killing the man on death row strapped to the chair didn't get pleasure from killing the man, but it was necessary. That was how Yip judged the man who broke the family's rules. He didn't take pleasure in ordering a man's death, but sometimes it was necessary. Red learned from that example and he hoped he'd never be in a position where he had to enforce that rule, but deep down, he knew it was likely.

CHAPTER 6

Renovations were ongoing in Red's Starlight Club, and while the bar wouldn't be open for another two weeks, the restaurant wouldn't be open to the public for at least another three months, maybe longer. The ballroom would remain closed until they could renovate it the way Red wanted it.

Red was in his office going over the books when a knock on the door interrupted him. "Come on in," Red bellowed, and Pissclam entered. "What do you want, Pissclam?"

"I don't want nothin', boss, but there's a Mrs. Genera here to see you."

"I don't know a Mrs. Genera. Did she say what she wanted to see me about?"

"No, boss."

Red shook his head, annoyed at the interruption. "Okay, show her in." Red stacked the papers he was working on and he put them aside, and when Pissclam ushered Mrs. Genera into his office. Red greeted her. "Have a seat, Mrs. Genera, and tell me what you wanted to see me about." Mrs. Genera looked to be in her mid to late thirties, and Red could tell that she was once a beautiful woman. She still had a good figure, and although she was still a very attractive woman, she seemed tired and her looks were fading, maybe due to hard work, and the stress of raising her family, and never getting enough money from her hard-working husband to pay the rent and other bills. Red studied the nervous woman sitting before him. She was on the verge of tears. He motioned to Pissclam standing near the open door. "Bring Mrs. Genera a cup of coffee and a shot of brandy."

"Okay, boss," Pissclam said as he rushed to the bar to fetch coffee and the brandy.

"Now tell me what you wanted to see me about, Mrs. Genera. Take your time. I assure you I don't bite," he said with a disarming smile, using his charm to relax the nervous woman.

"I feel stupid coming to see you, Mr. Fortunato."

"Please call me Red... and what's your first name, Mrs. Genera?"

"Forgive me Mr., uh, Red, my name is Gloria."

"Relax, Gloria. Like I just said... I don't bite. Now please continue with what you were telling me."

"I came here to see you because I didn't know who else to talk to." She hesitated for a moment, as if she was embarrassed or reluctant to continue the conversation, but Red's question forced her to answer.

"Talk to me about what, Mrs. Genera?"

She took a deep breath and sighed. "It's my fourteen-year-old son, Tommy. He attends P.S. 16. I'm afraid for him, Mr. Fortunato. While his friends remain in school for another class, because of his schedule, Tommy gets out of school a little early. When he comes home, lately, he's been very nervous. When I asked him what was wrong, at first he just shrugged his shoulders and said nothing, but yesterday, he told me a man followed him from school, and the man scared him."

Red had an idea what the man's intention toward her son could be, but he said nothing about that. "Does this man follow your son every day, or was this a onetime incident?"

"Tommy told me this man has followed him home for the past three days. Yesterday, the man propositioned him. He said he'd pay Tommy for an hour of his time. Tommy asked him what he'd have to do for the money, and the man told him that all he'd have to do was to accompany him to Flushing Meadows Park, where they could be alone. That was all my son had to hear. Without another word, he turned, and he ran home, and that's when he told me about the man. He told me he was frightened, and he didn't know what to do, and to be honest with you, it frightened me too. My husband works, but he was willing to lose a day's work to confront this man, but I talked him out of it because we couldn't afford to lose the day's pay. That's when I came here and talk to you. If I got to speak to

The Sicilian Caper

you, I promised myself that I'd do what I'm doing now, and ask you to help us."

"What you're asking me to do is not in my line of work, Gloria. I run a bar and restaurant. But the truth is I don't like to see kids stalked by a perverted predator, so I sympathize with you." Red gave the woman a blank slip of paper. "Write your name, telephone number, and your address on this paper. If you have a description of this man, then write that down too. One more thing. Do you have a picture of your son with you?"

"Yes, I do." She opened her purse and took out a photo of her son. "This is a recent picture of my son Tommy."

Red studied the photo, and when she finished writing, he studied the information, but took his time reading the description of the pervert. "Very good, Mrs. Genera. I'll look into this and I'll call you the moment I have something to share with you, but you left out what the best time would be to reach you."

"I'm sorry Red. I'm a housewife, so you can call me whatever time is best for you."

"One more thing, Gloria. It won't pay for my associates to miss your son when he gets out of school, so I must know, when he leaves school, is it on the 42nd Street side or the 41st Street side of the school?"

"The 41st Street side, Red."

"Good! I appreciate you coming here to see me with your problem. I don't like to hear from women worrying about their children's safety. I'll look into it and I promise, we'll put a stop to it. Now, is there anything else I can do for you?"

"No, Red. Thank you for seeing me." Red picked up the slip of paper and studied her address. "You live on 42nd Avenue. If you're nervous, I can have one of my men walk you home."

"That's unnecessary, Red. It's the middle of the day and I don't think that man is interested in a woman. His interests are with young boys."

"Thank you for coming in to see me, Mrs. Genera. You'll be hearing from me."

"Please, Red, it's Gloria."

Red smiled charmingly. "Gloria it is, then. Goodbye for now, Gloria. It was nice talking with you."

Red waited until she left his club, and then he called Pissclam into his office. "You wanted to see me, boss?"

"Yes. I have a job I want you to handle. Take Jimmy the Hat with you and go to PS 16 Jr. High School. That's the school up the street near 104th Street. Be there at 2 pm." Red explained the situation and what he wanted Pissclam to do. "I don't want this pervert to see you two, until you nab him, then scare the daylights out of him. Rough him up a little, but don't get carried away and kill the guy. Just scare the hell out of him, and make sure he **gets** the message that he's to leave young boys alone. Tell him that if I find out he's still hitting on young boys, his days of being a sick fairy will be over... permanently."

At 4 pm sharp, there was a knock on Red's door.

"Who is it?"

"It's me, and Jimmy, boss."

"Come on in, Pissclam." Both Pissclam and Jimmy the Hat walked in and sat down opposite Red's desk. "Did the guy show up?" Red asked.

"Yeah, he showed up. We picked him up just as he was about to approach the kid. Jimmy shoved him in the backseat and sat beside him. We drove to the Ridgewood warehouse. As soon as we walked in, we shoved the sick bastard into an empty office and sat him down. Then I put the barrel of my gun to his forehead and, as serious as I could so he would understand, I told him if you so much as approach Tommy or any young boys in our neighborhood again, you'll be signing your death warrant. I let him know I wanted to kill him, but my orders were to just give him a warning. The poor bastard wet himself."

Red chuckled. "Good. I'm glad you just scared the hell out of him and you didn't hurt him. Do you think he bought the warning?" Red asked.

Pissclam nodded. "He got the message after I bitch-slapped him a few times, and when I did that, the chicken-shit fairy cried like a little baby. And I mean cry, but you know what I think, boss?"

"No... what do you think, Pissclam?"

"I think he meant it when he said he wouldn't bother boys anymore. But, and this is only my opinion, boss. I think he won't be able to help himself. When enough time passes, being

The Sicilian Caper

what he is... he'll begin propositioning young boys again. Only next time, he'll be more careful, but it's in his nature to do it again. Nah, my thinking is he won't stop."

Red gave Pissclam a tight-lipped smile, agreeing with his assessment of the guy. "We gave the sick bastard a firm warning. We warned him what would happen if he hit on another young boy again... and he knows that next time there will be consequences." Red lit a cigar, took a puff, and asked Pissclam a last question before dismissing him. "Did Tommy see you grab the queer and put him in the back seat?"

"Yeah. Tommy is young, and he's scared to death of this guy, but, yeah, he saw Jimmy shove the miserable bastard in the car's backseat. When we took him to our Ridgewood warehouse and I got his attention, I told him what would happen to him if we found out he was still trying to seduce young boys in the neighborhood."

"Did he say or do anything after you roughed him up?"

"The bum pissed his pants. So we handcuffed him to the chair and let him sit alone for about an hour in the empty warehouse while we sat in an office behind him where he couldn't see us, but we could keep our eyes on him. After about an hour, we unlocked the handcuffs and took him back to Corona. We warned him again about what would happen to him if he didn't heed our warning. The guy was shaking like a leaf. He couldn't believe his luck when we got back to Corona and let him out of the car unhurt. He thought when we brought him to the warehouse, we were going to kill him"

"I'm glad you didn't kill the sick fuck. With a witness watching you, it could've come back to haunt us. I'll call Gloria Genera to let her know she can stop worrying about numb-nuts bothering her son any longer. That sick pervert understands what will happen to him if he disregards the warning we gave him and bothers her son again." Red looked at his two men. "You know, I don't give a shit what someone does behind closed doors, but it bothers the hell out of me to have them flaunt their way of life in front of me. Keep it to yourself and I don't give a shit what or who you are, just don't go waving what you are in front of me. I don't do it to you, and I don't want you doing it to me. If the guy found a like-minded person and did

39

what he had to do in private, I wouldn't care 'cause it's none of my business what two people do behind closed doors. Just don't shove what you do in my face."

"I feel the same way, boss," Pissclam added, with Jimmy nodding his head in agreement.

When Pissclam and Jimmy the Hat left, Red picked up the phone and called Gloria Genera. She picked up on the first ring. Red wasn't one to stay long on the phone because of his ever present concern that they could have tapped his phones. He kept it short, telling her they talked to the man who approached her son, and with a little persuasion, the man promised he wouldn't bother Tommy again, but he cautioned, "If in the future anyone approaches your son, I want you to call me immediately." Red hung up, and he sat back in his comfortable leather desk chair, feeling better, having helped a worried mother concerned about a pervert bothering her young son.

Gloria Genera hung up the phone and shuddered, grasping what Red must have meant when he casually told her that "after a little persuasion," that man wouldn't bother Tommy any longer.

CHAPTER 7

Red's old safe-cracker friend Ernie advised Red to do what the new casinos in Vegas were doing. The two men spent hours discussing the pros and cons of using color in the casino's bar and grill. Using color as an emotional stimulant was a relatively new and radical concept. Psychologists studied how colors could affect a person and how to use colors properly to increase an establishment's profit. They concluded that the walls, ceiling, and floors of a gambling establishment should have cool, soothing colors and dim lights, and the walls and rugs lining the floors should be bathed in cool dark purples and blue colors, which subconsciously made a player want to linger a while longer, to remain there in no rush to leave... just yet. Conversely, studies showed that restaurants should have hot red, orange, and yellow colors on the seats, tables, walls and floors, because studies concluded fiery colors work on a person's subconscious level. The hot colors made customers rush to leave the restaurant and not linger longer than necessary after they finished their meal. So Red had the bar bathed in cool colors and the result was a bar that differed completely from what Red had originally envisioned. The total effect was far more low key and more impressive than Red expected.

After the Starlight Club's bar was finished, Red studied the completed room, and it looked extremely inviting. He knew that if he felt comfortable seated at the bar, then a customer should also feel comfortable sitting at the bar, or at one table snuggled against the wall by a window. He returned to his office and picked up the papers he was working on, but after a few minutes, he placed them back on his desk. He leaned back in his plush leather desk chair and thought about the warning

Jeannie Leg-and-a-half gave him. He envisioned what Red's Place would have looked like when they completed it. Red pictured his original idea, and he liked it. Then he thought of what he had here in this bar & grill. He realized now how limited Red's Place would have been when compared to this place. *Things happen for a reason*, he thought. Here he could have three hundred people, plus another twenty or thirty at the front bar. He could never have done that at Red's Place, and besides, Ziggy needed a place to work out of, to hold his meetings, pay his crew, and that old wreck of a place, when they rebuilt it, it would provide an additional income for him. Red knew it would be perfect for Ziggy.

Red thought about what he wanted to do with this place. He could picture the completed Starlight Club and if Artie understood what Red wanted the place to look like, and build the Starlight Club exactly as Red envisioned it, he'd not only have a world class eatery and nightclub, but a world famous popular landmark that would attract tourists. He knew what he wanted to accomplish in the future, but he told no one, not even Trenchie. His plans included Las Vegas casinos, a movie studio in Hollywood, and other investments, but he kept those thoughts to himself. His plans were his and only his. Then he thought of that pretty young lady, Jeannie-Leg-And-A-half's ominous warning she warned Red about. Half of the warning came true. They destroyed Red's Place, but just as she predicted, he wasn't hurt. It was the second warning that troubled him. She predicted it would happen in the future. His famous place… and those were her words. His famous place would be blown up, and Red would be badly injured, but he would recover from his injuries.

1961, Trenchie's Return

The days and months passed fast for Red, but for the person spending time in the Big Q, or even at the lighter country club atmosphere of Danbury Federal prison that Doc had gotten him transferred to, the days still passed slowly. But knowing the day of his release was quickly approaching brought a smile to Trenchie's prison-hardened face. In two weeks, he'd be a free

The Sicilian Caper

man. He couldn't wait for his release, and since he served his full ten years, he wouldn't have to worry about his parole. He'd be a free man in every sense of the word. He looked forward to seeing the guys, because the only guys that visited him were Red and Ernie. Tarzan came a few times, and Yip visited him twice in San Quentin and once in Danbury. He missed the action and the guys, and now that he was a short-timer, he couldn't wait to be released.

In the intervening ten years, the renovations to the Starlight Club's bar and entrance made it unrecognizable from its original look. The bar was a long bar originally made of the finest wood. So it wasn't a problem for the carpenters to sand off and dig through the many layers of finish accumulated over the decades, and then refinish the wood, giving it a modern look. They installed modern mirrors with indirect lighting on the wall behind the bar, giving the customer the notion that the bar was twice as large as it really was. They replaced the large, patterned tin sheets covering the ceiling it with a beautiful new ceiling. They set hundreds of tiny, recessed lights into the black ceiling, giving the room the illusion that flickering ever-changing colors from the stars were crowding the dark sky above. The shimmering lights shone comfortably down from above, which made customers comfortable, giving them the feeling that they wanted to linger a little longer and didn't want to leave just yet.

They released Trenchie from prison two days earlier than his release date, so no one knew to pick him up. Instead, he took a taxi. Shortly after his release, a lowlife punk by the name of Rags assassinated Yip and his two bodyguards.

* * *

"Did you take care of the rat bastard?" Joey Boy asked.

Red, always fearing being recorded, just nodded. He grabbed Joey Boy's arm and pulled him close enough to whisper in his ear, "The stupid bastard was at Ziggy's, drunk as a skunk, bragging about how he still could build a bomb. Ziggy gave him stiff drinks to keep him there, and then he sent someone to tell me he had the guy who built the bomb. The man Ziggy sent told me Ziggy and his men would keep the guy there at his place, but he wanted me to come to his club as soon as possible, which I did. I dropped everything and rushed to Ziggy's place in Corona Heights. I don't have to draw you a picture of what happened to the bum after I got my hands on him. As Ernie would have said... the bastard died of shortness of breath."

Red's story fascinated Joey Boy. "Did you whack the guy right there in Ziggy's place?"

"No. He was so drunk, he didn't know where he was, so we took him to the Starlight Club and tied him to a chair in the cellar. Then we waited for him to wake up."

"So what happened when Rags woke up?"

"I needed to know who paid him to make the bomb that killed Yip, so when he woke up, I questioned him."

"Did he talk?"

"He told me everything. The guy thought that if he cooperated with me, I would give him a pass. So even though I never said I would, he thought he could buy his life by spilling everything with me."

"Did he tell you who paid him to kill Yip?"

"Yeah. It was Profaci, and when I heard him say that, I made myself a promise to whack that cheap prick."

Even though Joey Boy was one of Red's most trusted men, Red knew he said too much. "Raise your arms, Joey Boy."

"What?"

"You heard me. Raise your arms." Joey Boy slowly raised his arms. His expression was one of confusion. Red patted him down to make sure he wasn't wearing a wire. "Okay, you can put your hands down now."

"Geez, boss, I can't believe you don't trust me. I'd never agree to wear a wire."

"Don't take it personal, Joey Boy. It's just that I can't take any chances with anyone, and that goes for you too. I told you more just now about things better left unsaid than I've told anyone but Trenchie. I like you, Joey Boy, but liking someone has no place in our line of work, and that goes for you too. If you want to live a long life, be careful who you confide in, because the person you tell your secrets to now will be your executioner in the future. Remember, three people can keep a secret if two of them are dead." He gave Joey Boy a dark look. "That's Big Red's philosophy, and the motto he lives by. I made a mistake just now, telling you things I have told no one. Things that could get me locked up, or even worse, get me killed. The feds would love to hear what I just told you. You know... I'm the only major crime boss that they haven't turned the key on yet, and believe me, they'd have a holiday if they could put me behind bars."

Joey Boy realized he went a little too far in asking Red how he started in the business. He couldn't help himself and he asked Red a last question. "Red, earlier you said there were two shooters that killed your father, is that right?"

"Yeah, that's right... and?"

"I was told you got one guy, but what happened to the second shooter? Did you get him?"

"No, the guy is slippery. He sneaks into the country and he knows the truck we're going to hit almost before we know it. To protect the trucks, I had men riding shot-gun in a car behind the trucks, but as soon as I do that, one of my bookmakers gets hit. I hate to say this, but with the slick way the robberies have gone down, it makes sense to me, the information is coming from someone on the inside." Red caught the look on Joey Boy's face, and he smiled. "Relax, Joey Boy. I know the inside man isn't you, so relax. In fact, from this moment on, you have a new job. You're going to be my eyes and ears, because I want you to find out who's feeding Enzo the information he's getting about my operation. Enzo strikes on average once, maybe twice a year, but it's costly because he'll hit a truck we hijacked or plan to hijack and he'll take the inventory, which is worth a small fortune. We only hit the trucks carrying quality goods, like expensive fur coats, or expensive men's suits, or high-end women's gowns and dresses. Some trucks we hit carry expensive watches or televisions. We only hit certain trucks carrying high-end products, and there's no guesswork because we too have an inside man. I've made many truck drivers rich men. Those drivers are part of my mob. They only contact me if they're scheduled to carry a high-end load. At a pre-selected location, they'll stop and have lunch. During their lunch, one of my men will get in the truck, grab the keys from the visor, start the big rig up, and drive it to a pre-selected drop off. The client is waiting for his product. I pay my man in cash after the product is unloaded. Then he drives the truck to a certain location, and that's where he leaves the big rig. He gets in the follow-up car and they drive away. Now how can Enzo know what day and which truck will be targeted? He can't possibly know, because A) he's in Sicily, and B) we keep the targeted truck secret, and besides me, we keep the date of the take-down and the truck secret, and only to a few of my select men know the facts. Do you remember when I patted you down, feeling for a wire?"

"Yes. I remember."

"Do you remember how you felt?"

"Yeah, I remember. It was a very uncomfortable feeling."

"Good. I'm glad you remembered. I'm going to give you a list of men who would have known the day, date, time, truck, cargo, and lunch stop. I want you to do to them what I did to you, and by that I don't mean checking if they're wearing a wire. I mean, even though I trust them, I want you to overlook that fact and look at them as potential informants. If those men whose names are on the list are not the informants, then find the man who is the rat, and bring me his name."

"Wow, Red. Finding out who the informant is a big order. I'm just a soldier in your organization. I know nothing about investigating and trying to discover who the informant is."

Red raised his hands in mock surrender and grinned. "Hell, Joey Boy. I never expected you to put on your shining armor, take your lance, and get on your white horse, and then charge to a castle and challenge the bad guy holding the princess to a joust. I'm giving you help. I've briefed Ernie on the situation, and I told him to postpone his trip to Vegas and drop anything else he's doing, because he's going to help you find the guy who ratted on us. Now Ernie may be an old timer, and even though he seems like a mug, he's an intelligent thinker, and he's become an analyst through many years of experience, and he's as sharp as they come. That's why Ernie has survived in this racket as long as he has. If he offers you any insight or suggestions, you listen to him, understand?"

The Sicilian Caper

"I understand, boss, but can I ask you a question?"

"Sure, ask."

"Ernie's not Italian, he's German, and I like the guy. I was wondering what he was doing with the Gallo brothers mob... and why did you allow him to join your crew?"

"Ernie's an old safe-cracker with an interesting history that dates back to before the second World War, which it directly involved him in."

"How was he involved, Red?"

"He knew a man who was a doctor, and he owned a tract of land in Argentina. The land was an anomaly. It had several special features that were important to the United States war effort. It had extensive rubber plants, which the government needed badly. It also had a variety of nuts and fruits, and they found an abundance of gold and silver on the land. The rubber on Ernie's land was accessible just a few yards from the water through an inlet. Ernie petitioned the government and tried to interest them, but no dice. They refused."

"Why? What happened?"

"Politics happened. A prominent politician convinced the government to buy the land he represented, which had to be dredged a mile and an expensive half, in order to get to the rubber. But that was the land the United States government bought, and not Ernie's... and all because of a politician who was politically connected. Politicians!... Don't get me started on them.

"After that, Ernie wound up working for Jimmy Hines, who was the power behind the governor of New York. A few years later, he got in a bit of trouble when he and Tarzan started charging twenty-five cents tax on every vending machine brought into New York State. The government arrested both of them and brought them to trial in Mineola, Long Island. They wound up having the most expensive trial in Mineola's history. Jimmy Hoffa paid all of their expenses and he sent his personal lawyer, Bennet Williams, to defend them. When the trial ended, both Ernie and Tarzan wound up spending ten years in prison, and right now, I consider Ernie the most important member of my crew. It's too bad he's not Italian, because he would be a made man. But he understands the rules, and he's okay with it.

Now, do you have any more questions?"

"No, Red."

"Good. Now Ernie will be here soon. Wait for him, and then go find me the informer."

CHAPTER 8

Madonie Mountains, North of Mt. Aetna

Enzo paced restlessly back and forth in the cave he had been living in since returning to the Madonie region in Sicily. He had plenty of American money stashed in his cave. The money came from the trucks and the book-making parlors he robbed over the years from Red. Enzo had developed a small, greedy network of fences he sold his goods to that never knew the goods they were buying were Red's, or if they did, they never let on that they knew. If Big Red Fortunato discovered who was buying his stolen merchandise, the fences' lives as they knew it would quickly end. The problem with Enzo had been he couldn't remain in New York for any length of time. Every move he made had to be timed, or in movie parlance, he would have had to storyboard his moves. Once his snatch and grab of Red's goods had been successful, he had to disappear quickly, in order not to be caught, and that had been working for him these many years since they forced him to leave town after mistakenly killing Red's father. Enzo had learned to become a ghost. Someone who, within hours of arriving in Queens, put his plans in motion. If, for some unforeseen reason, they delayed his plans for even an hour, he'd forego his plans to hurt Red and return to the safety of his Sicilian mountain hideout. He was at peace there because no one knew where he was, and trying to find him was nearly impossible. Sicilian fir and manna ash surrounded the cave he hid out in, and only someone who was born and brought up in the area around the Madonie Mountains might know of the secret caves that were hidden behind the lush green fir and ash trees. But there were so many caves in the Madonie Mountain region, it would have taken a bloodhound to find him. Enzo regretted killing Red's father. It was an accident, a mistake that caused him the enmity of Vito Genovese, Yip, and Big Red Fortunato, and Enzo had been paying for his mistake for these many years. He blamed Red and not Vito Genovese, who paid him to kill a sworn enemy of his. But Enzo killed the wrong man, which caused the two men, Vito Genovese and Yip, to put a contract on Enzo Batto. But the man he blamed most was Big Red, for forcing him to leave the United States, and he believed, as most Sicilians do... in the vendetta. In the ensuing years, he swore to have his revenge on big Red, and he did everything in his power to destroy the Queens mobster.

The problem Enzo faced was Big Red was so powerful, and he had such a large criminal organization, when he returned to Queens, and robbed one of Red's trucks or one of his betting parlors, it was like swatting a fly. Where there were that many flies, if you killed one fly, you hardly noticed it, but money talked, and through the years, he'd stolen enough of Red's money to make him a rich man, so he kept on robbing the Queens mobster, his sworn enemy. With the money he made from robbing Red's illegal businesses, Enzo bought a few of Red's low level soldiers. He hit the jackpot with one particular mobster. The man proved invaluable to Enzo, as long as he received his envelope with the agreed-upon amount of cash in it, which had to be delivered before the man would divulge when and where the next truck could be hi-jacked, or when a particular bookie had a safe load of money ready to be taken.

Enzo picked up his special address book and scanned the pages for one particular name, a name that made him wealthy. Nicky "Sneakers" Carbone. Carbone was a soldier in Ziggy's crew, and his penchant for designer sneakers gave him his nickname. He could betray Red and his fellow mobsters because his brother-in-law, Johnny Varick, was the senior dispatcher for United Trucking, a large trucking firm headquartered on the west side of Manhattan. United Trucking hauled beef, furs, electronic items, men's suits, and various other valuable commodities, and that was the man who tipped Nicky Sneakers with the date, time, and destination a truck with a valuable cargo would pull out of the United Trucking

The Sicilian Caper

terminal.

When Enzo first invited Nicky Sneakers to lunch on a windy Thursday in March at a remote restaurant in upstate New York, Nicky refused. But two days later, he received an envelope with a second invitation. In the envelope with the invitation was a short note, and this time, he agreed to meet with Enzo. His motivation for accepting Enzo's invite was on the short note were ten one-hundred-dollar bills paper-clipped to the note. The note had an address on one side and written on the other side simply written was, "You will receive another ten one-hundred-dollar bills when we meet for lunch.

"I'll be wearing a blue suit, white tie, and white sneakers. When you see me, hand me the invitation so I know it is you. If you are interested, be at the hotel at the address on the invitation next Tuesday at 12 noon sharp. I'll wait for twenty minutes. If you are not there by then, I'll leave, and you won't hear from me again."

A week earlier, Enzo quietly flew into the **Wilkes-Barre/Scranton** International Airport and took a cab the thirty-eight miles to the hotel's address stated on the note. The hotel was near the Pocono Mountains. If he had chosen a hotel in the Poconos, he was afraid someone might recognize him, so instead he chose a hotel near the Pocono Mountains, but not too close to that popular resort.

Enzo was easy to spot. He was seated at a table in a private nook. Enzo's blue suit and white tie caused him to stand out like a lighthouse beacon on a dark sea. Nicky Sneakers' eyes slid down to the man's shoes, and when he saw that the man in the blue suit and white tie also wore white sneakers, he ambled over to his table and handed Enzo the invitation. Enzo didn't bother to check it; he just shoved it in his inside jacket pocket. "Have a seat," Enzo said, and Nicky sat down.

"Before we go any further, I believe you have something for me," Nicky said. Enzo smiled, reached in his jacket, slid an envelope out containing ten crisp one-hundred-dollar bills, and handed it to Nicky Sneakers.

"I always keep my word, and I always take care of my men. I hope when we leave here today, I can consider you one of my men."

The first ten one-hundred-dollar bills went a long way in interesting Nicky Sneakers to hear why Enzo invited him to lunch, and what he had in mind for him. After all, so far, he did pay him two thousand dollars to get him here, so how much more would he offer him... to do what? That was the question nagging at Nicky... to do what? What did this man want from him? He couldn't answer that question until he heard him out, but whatever he wanted from him he thought would cost the man dearly. So Nicky just nodded when Enzo suggested they order a light lunch before discussing business, which Nicky agreed to. Discussing money matters always gave him an appetite, and today was no different.

After lunch, Enzo suggested they go outside to the rear patio where it was more private. He didn't like discussing business in a crowded dining room, where there was always the possibility they could be heard. They found an unoccupied private table in a corner, and they sat down and enjoyed the cool mountain breeze. Enzo took two cigars from the leather cigar pouch he carried in his inside jacket pocket, and handed a cigar to Nicky. After lighting the cigars, Nicky continued. "Okay. I'll agree. The two grand was an impressive way to get me to a meeting. Now that I'm here, I'm waiting to hear why you wanted to meet with me." Nicky said this with a hint of a smile on his rugged face.

Enzo studied Nicky for a long moment, as if trying to decide where to begin, and how forthcoming he should be with him. He came straight to the point and told Nicky what he wanted from him. His eyes still looked on Nicky for a long uncomfortable moment, but if he thought he could rattle the guy, he was wrong, so he gave up, and instead he asked him, "How well do you know Big Red Fortunato?"

"Not well at all. Once in a while, he'll stop in to see my boss, but I never talked to him. I don't think he even knows I'm a part of his crew."

"That's good, because I need someone in his organization that I can trust and depend on, and is not important to him." Then Enzo added, "I'd like that someone to be you, Nicky, and if it is you, I'll make you a rich man."

Nicky nodded, but his face remained stoic. He didn't show

The Sicilian Caper

a bit of emotion. "Go ahead, I'm listening, and you still haven't told me anything."

"Fair enough." Enzo said. "Here's something you don't know. Someday I'm going to kill big Red, and that's a fact. But until that day comes, I intend to ruin him, and become very wealthy doing it. As it is, I've already become wealthy by taking a small part of what is his and making it mine. I can do better if I had an inside man like you helping me. Do you have anything against becoming a rich man?" he asked, knowing the answer.

"No, and I know I'll never become wealthy doing what I'm doing now."

"Are you interested in working with me, Nicky? If you come aboard, my plans are that no one but Big Red will get hurt, but before I kill him, I'll hurt Big Red in his pocket. Are you interested in joining me?"

It took a few seconds for Nicky to answer Enzo. It was as if was doing a few quick calculations. Finally, he answered. "You have said little so far, Enzo. Why don't you get straight to the point and tell me what you want from me? You paid two grand to get me here, which impressed me. I must admit, it was very creative… and expensive, so let's get to the heart of this deal. Tell me how I can help you, and what will you give me for that help?"

"All right. I'll level with you. I aim to hurt Big Red badly. I intend to rob the trucks he plans on hijacking before he does. Red makes a fortune every Wednesday with the horses he runs, and when he gets paid from the track, I plan on robbing that money from him too, but I need someone on the inside who can let me know what time the trucks carrying expensive goods, will roll, and I'll need to know what they're hauling, as well as their destination. My inside man will receive ten percent of each heist."

"Ten percent is not enough incentive to motivate me to go against Big Red. Make it twenty-five percent and you have a deal."

Enzo smiled inwardly through the pained expression he forced on his face. That was the exact amount Enzo had in mind for the inside man, but he hid his satisfaction, and instead he kept the pained expression on his face. Enzo smiled inwardly, but acted as if the twenty-five percent was way more than he intended to pay an inside man. Nicky Sneakers held his breath. He would settle for less, but he didn't want to give in to soon. To his surprise, Enzo accepted his demand. "You're lucky… I need an inside man right now, and I'm in a tight spot, so I'll give you the twenty-five percent you're asking for, but I'll only pay you on information you give me that I act on. Fair enough?"

Nicky Sneakers smiled, thinking he came out on top, but buried deep in his subconscious mind was the thought that if Big Red ever discovered he betrayed him, all he might have done just now was sign his death warrant, but he shook the thought from his mind and smiled. "Fair enough, Enzo," he said with an uncertain smile on his lips.

"Now that you agreed to work with me, the good news is we'll only work our deal once or twice a year, maybe only once every two years, but that one time will be very lucrative for us. If we get greedy and try to act more than once, we could get caught. It pays to keep Red guessing when we'll hit him. I believe in the KISS method."

"KISS method? What's that?" Nicky Sneakers asked.

Enzo grinned. "The KISS method is Keep It Simple, Stupid. By hitting Red once a year, you'll make more money than you would have if you worked every day that entire year, and by doing that, we'll be keeping it simple. I intend to keep Red guessing by hitting him once or maybe twice a year. If we hit him more than that, he may discern a pattern and outguess us, and him outguessing us is something I don't want to happen. Understand?"

Nicky nodded. "I understand and agree with you. It's better to be safe than sorry."

Enzo slapped Nicky on his shoulder. "That's right; we want to be wealthy, not sorry."

The two men shook hands, solidifying their arrangement, then they both sat back down and discussed how best they could implement their plans. One thing Enzo insisted on was that they come up with a safe way to contact one another. "It's one thing to know when a truck with the cargo we want is leaving the terminal, but getting that information to me with no one being

The Sicilian Caper

the wiser was another thing." Enzo had given his plan a lot of thought, and by the time he met with Nicky, he had it all pre-planned. Enzo had dissected all the ramifications of something going wrong and all the ways to communicate with one another before the meeting and he arrived at two solutions as best how to communicate. The first and more direct method of communicating was a phone call to a small tobacco shop in the little town of Gratteri at the base of the mountain where the shop owner was Enzo's first cousin, Mario Gratolli.

The second choice was to use the code he had used in the past. He handed Nicky Sneakers a slip of paper with a simple cypher written on it. That cypher was the secondary means of communicating with one another. If someone accidentally saw the message, they would not understand what the message conveyed. Using a cypher, or code, was the second method for the two men to communicate safely with one another. The problem with this method was that although they couldn't interpret the message easily, the message was still difficult to deliver to an associate. But a phone call at a precise time, to a little tobacco shop in the snug little town of Gratteri in Sicily to talk to a cousin, was nothing that would arouse suspicion that anything was amiss.

The quaint town of Gratteri was in the Madoni section of Sicily. They decided a phone call to Enzo at the tobacco shop was a preferable, and a much safer way for the two men to communicate with one another. For the following twelve years, the plan worked perfectly for both Enzo Batto and Nicky Sneakers. Once Johnny Varick, Nicky's brother-in-law, passed the information to Nicky, he passed the information to Enzo, and then Enzo acted on it. The result was after selling the goods to their fence, Enzo and his two partners made a small fortune. The buyer always knew when they would deliver the stolen merchandise to him, and when they delivered the merchandise, they would hand an attaché case full of cash to Enzo. Then the money would immediately be divided between the three men, and then without further discussion, Enzo stepped into Johnny Varick's Cadillac and then Johnny quickly drove Enzo to the airport. Then, after checking in with his pre-paid ticket non-stop to Sicily, Enzo boarded the plane, and he flew back to Palermo where no one could touch him. He breathed a sigh of relief when the plane touched down on the tarmac at the airport in Palermo. He was home now, and once Enzo was back in his cave, he knew he would be safe from Big Red's long reach.

Enzo was comfortable driving his mint ten-year-old black Mercedes the one hundred and ten miles from Palermo to Gratteri. He made one stop, and that was to visit the local mafia chieftain. Don Roberto Castillo.

The Don wasn't a big man, but he was built like a bull and he had a full head of wavy silver hair and a full mustache that gave him a rakish look. They searched Enzo and, since he wasn't armed, they escorted him into Don Roberto Castillo's office. Enzo bent his knees to the old Don, and he kissed his ring as a show of respect. "What did I do to deserve a visit from Enzo Batto, a man who never shows respect to me, unless he wants something from me? So what is it this time? What do you want now, Enzo?"

Enzo hesitated a moment before speaking. He took a deep breath and he let it out slowly, and then he looked the old man in the eye and said. "I need to hire two good men. Men who are competent and who are tough men I can rely on."

Don Castillo appeared to have expected his request. "You are worried that the American from Queens, New York will come for you. And you need two men, one to watch for him and the other to protect you in case he gets past the first man. Right"

Enzo was speechless. It was as if the old Don reached right into his mind and saw why he needed the two men.

Don Castillo smiled like the cat who ate the delicious mouse. "What? You think I don't hear things? You think that when they threaten someone from my region of Sicily, I won't hear about it? If you think that, then you are sadly misguided, and you are not the man I thought you were." The old Don raised his cigar and pointed it at Enzo. "You killed the man's father who hunts you. If I were him, you would be dead many years now. But because you are under my protection, I will agree to your request. I will give you two of my best men and you will pay for them. I know you have made a lot of money by taking money from your so-called enemy, money that is not yours. So you'll pay my men three hundred dollars each a week,

The Sicilian Caper

with one hundred dollars of that money taken from each man, which you will pay to me. That is a fair price, and you are getting my help and the services of my two men who have made their bones, and you're getting them at a bargain price. But if the men from America come to my home and ask to see me, then the price of my protection will get very expensive for you. Let's not think of things that may never happen. Let's cross that bridge when we come to it. Go home now, and tomorrow morning, my men will meet you at your cousin's store. Tell them what you want them to do, and they will do it, even if they must perform wet work. If that happens, you must call me right away, and I will send a clean-up crew to clean and dispose of the mess. But remember, one-third or one hundred dollars from the money you're paying each man, you will give to me. Consider it a matter of principle, a tithe to show respect." Enzo didn't like the idea of giving anyone a tithe, or paying the two men, and he hated the thought of giving Don Castillo a penny of his money. Still... when he thought about it, the price was a bargain for two professional mafioso hitmen to work for him, and he had money thanks to the robberies he pulled off through the years against Big Red Fortunato.

When Enzo arrived in Gratteri, he parked his car. When he stepped out, it felt as if he just stepped off of a cloud. Before attempting to open the door to his cousin's little tobacco shop, Enzo looked at his watch. It was still early, and he knew his cousin Mario should still be in his shop. He better be here, he thought with a flash of anger. He tried the door, and it opened. Enzo stepped in the shop and the sweet smell of his cousin's favorite pipe tobacco wafted through the shop. "Mario, are you in the back?"

Mario called out loudly. "Yes, yes, I'm coming." Seeing it was his cousin Enzo, he smiled. "I waited for you, but it was getting late and I didn't think you were coming tonight. How was your business trip, Enzo? Profitable, I hope."

"Business was good, and profitable, but I need you to come with me up the mountain to my cave, Mario." It wasn't a request; it was an order, and Mario knew it. He said nothing because he knew his cousin's temper, and how easily he angered. He didn't want to provoke him.

Mario looked at his cousin suspiciously. "At this time of night, you want me to come with you up the mountain to your cave, Enzo?"

"Yes!" Enzo said. His eyes flashed with anger momentarily, his anger flaring up more often than it usually did, but he suppressed it and gave his cousin a tight, caustic smile. "You are so suspicious, cousin. I just want you to ride up the mountain with me to my cave, so you can take the horse I'm borrowing from you back down the mountain. You do that for me, cousin?" Enzo glared at Mario.

Mario didn't enjoy being ordered around by anyone, even his hot-tempered cousin. "Why don't you ride the horse up the mountain to your cave and leave him there 'til morning?"

"If I do that, then someone might see the horse, and that someone may be someone I don't want to know that the owner of the horse is in the cave."

Mario was short, with shaggy white hair and a drooping walrus mustache. His tired large brown eyes had bags under them large enough to carry a handful of grapes. "I see what you mean, but, Enzo, conclude your business earlier so I can close my shop and go home to Maria and my two beautiful children. Children need their father to have dinner with them, and tuck them into bed. Now what am I going to tell Maria and my children when I am always late and I miss dinner with them on the days you return from America on a business trip?"

Enzo was tired and his temper flared more frequently when he was tired, but he controlled it once again. If it were anyone else but Mario, Enzo would have reacted differently. Instead, he reached into his pocket and took out his swollen bankroll and he peeled some bills off and waved them in front of his cousin. "Maybe this will help with Maria and the children." Enzo stopped waving the money, and he handed Mario a fistful of American currency. "Here, buy your ugly fat wife something that will make her forget you weren't home for dinner, and get your kids something nice, and be sure to tell them it is from their cousin Enzo. Now get the horses and let's go. I'm tired from my trip, and my temper is getting the better of me."

Mario's eyes lit up like a one-hundred-watt lamp. "*Madre mia*, but this is a lot of money, Enzo. Are you sure you can

The Sicilian Caper

afford to give me this much money?"

Enzo smiled darkly. Even though he was a brutally ruthless contract killer, he could be a different man to his cousin Mario, at least as different as his taciturn, vicious attitude allowed him to be. "I always say one favor deserves another favor, Mario. You did me a favor, so now I'm returning the favor. Come with me to my cave, and then before you go home to your fat, hard-working wife, get something nice for her, and your children."

It would have made Mario happier if Enzo hadn't mentioned that Maria was fat, which was a sore point for him, and Enzo knew it, and that was why he said it. But that was Enzo; he'd hurt you anyway he could, Mario thought. *He gives with one hand, and then he takes with the other.* Enzo could never be completely nice to anyone, especially his favorite cousin, who, although Mario would never admit it to anyone, was intimidated by Enzo. He even frightened him, although he would never admit it. Still, Mario knew where to draw the line with his cousin. It wouldn't do to push Enzo too far. Who knew how he would react, even to his favorite cousin, especially in the Sicilian mountains, where a body might never be found.

"Don Castillo is sending two good men to help me. They'll watch for strangers, especially strangers, inquiring about me. They'll be here at your store tomorrow morning, so get here early. I'll be here early too. If they arrive before I get here, tell them to be patient, and I'll be with them shortly."

"Why send two men? What are you afraid of, Enzo? Are you expecting trouble?"

"I'm always expecting trouble... and I'm not afraid of anything or anyone, so stop asking me foolish questions. I don't like it when people ask me stupid questions."

"I meant nothing by it, Enzo. It's just that I'm your cousin and I'm concerned about you." Mario wasn't concerned about Enzo, but he was concerned for himself, his wife, and his children. If people were looking for Enzo, they could come to his house, and if they did, and Enzo wasn't there, then who knew what they would do to him and his family. Mario wasn't a brave man, and if the men looking for his cousin threatened or tortured him, or hurt his wife, he would tell them the location of Enzo's cave, and he'd tell them anything else they wanted to know about him. The downside was he would tell the men what they wanted to know about his cousin, if that would prevent them from hurting him or his family, he knew if he did that, he'd have two problems... Enzo... and the men looking for him.

CHAPTER 9

Red was on the phone when Pissclam walked into his office and placed his morning coffee on his desk. Instead of leaving, he remained by his desk and waited for Red to hang up. Red cupped his phone. "Was there something else you wanted to see me about, Pissclam?"

"Yeah, boss, but it can wait until you're off the phone."

"All right... wait outside until I finish my phone call, and then I'll see you."

"Thanks, boss. I'll wait at the bar."

A little while later, Red stepped out of his office and waved at Pissclam to get his attention. When he saw Red motioning to him, he left his coffee on the bar and joined Red in his office. "What did you want to see me about, Pissclam?"

"I have some bad news, boss. Another of United Trucking's trucks got hit last night."

"Is the driver all right?"

"Yeah, he's fine, boss. Two men wearing face masks held guns on him when he came out of a diner and was about to get in his truck. One man held his gun on him while his partner got in his truck and drove it away. As soon as the truck turned the corner, his partner motioned with his gun for him to get in the car. He kept him in the car for a half hour, and all the while, he kept his gun on him. Then he told the guy to get out. 'Go back in the diner and wait ten minutes before you call the cops. If you call them sooner, I'll kill you.' The driver watched the man cross the street and enter the diner, and as soon as the door closed behind him, he drove away."

"Did the truck driver get the license plate?"

"Yes, boss. He was in the diner by the window, but as the

man drove away, he was close enough to see the plate clearly, so he quickly wrote the plate number on a napkin, and while he waited for his food, he called the police and he told them what happened, and he gave the plate number to the police. He remained on the phone while the police called the DMV. Here's the bad part, boss. When the police had the DMV do a search, they discovered the plate was from a car that was reported stolen from a commercial parking lot that same morning."

Red nodded, and he calmly took a sip of his coffee before placing the cup back on his desk. "I expected nothing less, Pissclam. Those men were professionals, and they knew what they were doing. These bums are clever. They cover their tracks, they choose their targets carefully, and amateurs do not do the robberies. They're getting their information from someone in our organization. I hope Ernie and Joey Boy find out who the informer is because the last person he'll see alive will be me." Red paced back and forth a few times in front of his desk as if he were thinking of various scenarios. He stopped and pointed at Pissclam. "The bum knows what truck we're planning to hit, so they hit a different truck carrying a load of valuable items. But they somehow out-think us. If we plan on robbing a truck, they either rob an unfamiliar truck or they rob one of our bookmakers. But whoever they rob, they already know they'll hit the jackpot, because whoever they hit, they'll come away with an incredible payday. Then they disappear into the woodwork."

***

The next day, Red noticed Joey Boy and Ernie standing at the front entrance to the club waiting for him.

"Did you find the informer or anything useful?"

"I think we found the guy, Red, but before we did anything to the guy, we wanted to speak to you first."

"Good. I'm glad to see you're using your head. Now what did you find out?"

Joey Boy tilted his head in Ernie's direction. "If we find that Ernie's hunch paid off, then you can thank him. We were getting nowhere, when Ernie changed tactics. Instead of going

The Sicilian Caper

in blind and not knowing what we were looking for, Ernie narrowed it down by asking your capos one question, which was the right question. He started asking if any of the guys bought a new car recently, or maybe a piece of expensive jewelry, and when we got to Ziggy and asked him those questions, we hit pay dirt. It seems that one of the guys buys a new Caddy every other year, and on his wrist, he's sporting a solid gold Rolex with a diamond bezel."

"What's the guy's name?"

"Nicky Carbone, goes by the name of Nicky Sneakers."

Red smiled grimly. "Yeah, I know the guy. He's one of Ziggy's men, and most of the time, he hangs around at Ziggy's bar and grill."

"What do you want to do about the guy, Red?"

"Pick him up and bring him here. When you get here, take him down into the cellar."

"But what if he's innocent, Red? What if he's not our informer?"

"We'll find out for sure after you bring him here. Now go get him. If he's not there, then wait for him until he does get there. Then bring him here. I can't wait to question the guy; now get out of here and find the guy and bring him here."

Ernie and Joey Boy sat at a table by the window in Ziggy's joint for four hours waiting for Nicky Sneakers, when a Caddy convertible pulled up to the curb in front of Ziggy's. "I never met the guy. Is that him?" Ernie asked.

"Yeah, that's him all right. Come on, let's meet him outside where we can get him before he enters the joint. It'll be easier to handle him outside than in here," Joey Boy said. Ernie agreed. Both men stood and quickly rushed to the door just as Nicky was about to enter. Joey Boy pressed his gun against Nicky's gut. "Leave your car where it is and get in the back seat of the black Ford Galaxy," Joey said, pointing to the Ford. "We're going to take a short ride."

"A short ride where?" Nicky said, shaking, his eyes wide with fear.

"You'll find out. Now get in the car."

Ziggy watched the scene unfold from a window near the bar. *Stupid fool,* he said to himself, shaking his head, then he turned and walked back into his office still shaking his head, thinking of the damned fool who traded his life for a few bucks.

It was a short seven-minute ride to the Starlight Club where Big Red waited in the dimly lit cellar. The cellar was as different from the Starlight Club as night was from day. The Starlight Club was modern and beautiful internationally famous club known for its beauty. It was a showcase that Red was extremely proud of. The cellar, on the other hand, was quite different from what was created above it. It remained unchanged from when it was first built back in the eighteen hundreds. It still had gas pipes lined in rows throughout the cellar with small on/off hand grips at spaced intervals to turn the gas in the pipes on and off. Upstairs, the Starlight Club was enchanting, while the cellar reminded one of a dark, dank, forbidding tomb. Red, Trenchie, Ralph, and Pissclam waited with their boss for Ernie and Joey Boy to escort Nicky Sneakers down the stairs for his appointment with Red. Tic-Tok came halfway down the stairs. "They just pulled up, boss."

"Good. Tell Ernie and Joey to bring Sneakers down here."

"Okay, boss. I'll tell them." Tic-Tok turned and hastened to the front bar to relay Red's message to his two men that they bring Nicky down to the cellar. Minutes later, Nicky sat in an uncomfortable kitchen chair, surrounded by a few of Red's hard, unforgiving men. Nicky Sneakers looked around at the men in the dimly lit cellar milling around him. He saw the unemotionless face of Big Red. Ralph was seen from his peripheral vision. It wasn't good news for Nicky if Ralph was there, and he was definitely there. Trenchie and Pissclam stood on his right side on the other side of the cellar stairs.

"Tell me why you betrayed me, Nicky?"

"Red, this is all a mistake. I didn't betray you. What makes you think I betrayed you?"

"You informed on me... And your friends by tipping off Enzo on which trucks would be hauling valuable merchandise, and you also told him which of our horse parlors had a safe full of cash for him to stick up."

Nicky Sneakers was shaking like a leaf, and no matter how hard he tried to control the shaking, it didn't work; in fact, the shaking appeared to get worse. "Cooperate, Nicky, talk to me.

The Sicilian Caper

Tell me everything, and I'll go easy on you. You will talk, Nicky, that I can guarantee you... You will tell me everything I want to know. Save yourself a lot of unnecessary pain, because I promise you, you will experience pain like you never thought possible. I'll give you an idea of what will happen to you if you don't tell me everything. The first thing that will happen is Ralph will take his razor-sharp stiletto and cut a small slit in your gut, just large enough to reach a finger into your stomach, and he'll pull out your intestines. You'll see him pour lighter fluid on your intestines and then he'll light them on fire. You'll watch your guts fry until they are blackened and crisp. Then, while your guts cool off, I will lock you in that room back there. But you'll be tied up and secured so you can't move, and you'll watch rats feast on your guts. That's what's about to happen to you if you don't tell me what I want to know."

Nicky Sneakers looked into the unforgiving faces of the men he betrayed and knew that Red was serious as a heart attack. He'd do exactly what he said he would do to him. Red studied his face looking for a sign of him weakening. A period of silence from Nicky caused the men to question whether or not he would talk, but finally, just before Red was about to tell Ralph, who was testing the sharpness of his stiletto's blade, to begin his grisly procedure, Nicky raised his head. "All right, I'll talk, but only if you promise not to torture me, and you keep your word to go easy on me."

Red slapped him on his shoulder. "Good man. I'm glad to hear you say you'll talk, because I would rather have killed you with a gunshot than watch Ralph pull your intestines out inch by inch so the rats could feast on your guts. Now tell me everything, and don't leave anything out. I'll know when you're lying and when you're telling me the truth. So let's hear just the truth part."

Nicky Sneakers told Red how Enzo contacted him by sending him an envelope with a note of instructions in it with ten one-hundred-dollar bills attached to the note. He explained how the note said there would be another ten one-hundred-dollar bills waiting for him when he arrived at the meeting. "How could I refuse another one thousand dollars, Red? I went to the meeting for the money, never expecting to agree to do anything for the guy."

Red gave him a tight-lipped smile. "You didn't expect to accept his deal, yet you accepted his deal, didn't you? You didn't just accept his deal, you jumped at it. You saw a way to become wealthy pretty damn quick, and you jumped at the opportunity."

"I just wanted to make a lot of serious money quickly, and then get out of the life. Maybe open up a little business with money coming in, and I wouldn't have to worry about an income in my old age."

Red's eyes narrowed and he glared coldly at Nicky. "Yeah, I know what you mean. It'd be nice to put away some money for your old age, like buying a new Caddy every other year, and a gold Rolex. You really know how to put money away for your old age, don't you? Have you tried applying to a college and then teach your students your method of saving money?

"I want to know the name of the guy you're working with, the guy who tips you off on which trucks are carrying expensive loads?"

"Now tell me your contact."

"My brother-in-law Johnny Varick is the dispatcher for United Trucking Corp. He knows I'm connected, but he doesn't know anything about who is robbing the trucks. He thinks I give the information to you and you act on it. I let him think what he wants to think and he's happy as a pig in shit when he gets the money I hand him."

"Write your brother-in-law's name, and address on this pad, and include his phone number and then hand the pad back to me, and what about Enzo? Tell me where I can find him."

"I don't know where he's hiding. All I know is he rushes back to Sicily soon after a robbery. He mentioned a mountain once, and he told me the name of the mafia chieftain, a Don Castillo. I remembered it because Castillo sounded like Castle, so it was easy to associate the two names. That's all I know, Red."

Having told Red everything he knew, Nicky Sneakers looked up hopefully at Red, hoping for a pass. "Red, I told you everything. I answered all of your questions, and you promised me that if I told you everything, you'd go easy on me. Please,

The Sicilian Caper

Red, let me go and I'll disappear and you'll never see me again."

"I know I told you that I'd go easy on you if you told me everything, and I have to admit, you kept your word, so I'll keep my word. I'll go easy on you." Red motioned to Ralph. "Ralph will drive you to your car."

Nicky had heard stories of Ralph and he knew his reputation. He knew if Ralph took him to his car, he was a dead man. He'd never make it to his car. "Please, Red. Let me walk to my car. The cool air will do me good. There's no need to bother Ralph. Besides, a walk would do me good."

"Look, Nicky. Don't argue with me. We drove you here, and we'll drive you back to your car." Nicky knew it was a one-way trip, so he decided he'd go out like the soldier he was. "All right, Red. I'll go with Ralph. I just want you to know that what I did wasn't personal. I got greedy, that's all, and in my greed, I let you down. Do me a favor and see that my sister gets my will. It's in my bedroom in the top drawer of my bureau. I left everything to her. You'll do that for me, won't you, Red?"

Red patted Nicky's shoulder as friends do. "Sure, Nicky. I'll do that for you. I'll see to it that your sister gets your will."

"Thanks, Red. I always liked you. You were a fair boss, and I made the mistake of letting greed overcome my good sense. I hope you get Enzo."

"I'm sorry it had to come to this, Nicky, because I liked you too, and it's too bad it had to end this way."

"Thanks, Red. I'm glad you feel that way." Nicky turned to leave, but he stopped and he turned and looked at Red. "See you in hell, boss." Nicky said with a wink and a sad smile.

"I'll see you when I get there, Nicky, and we'll talk about the good times." He tilted his head toward Ralph. "Take him to his car, Ralph."

"Okay, Red. Come on, Nicky, let's take a short ride."

When Nicky Sneakers walked up the cellar stairs with Ralph behind him, Pissclam asked Red, "Do you want me to take care of Nicky's brother-in-law Johnny Varick?"

"No! Don't touch him. When we get back from Sicily, I'm going to have a little talk with Varick. With Nicky gone, we'll use Varick. He's a valuable asset; he'll tip us off on which truck to hit instead of tipping off Nicky."

* * *

Once back in his office, Red motioned to Pissclam. "Is Tarzan working at the bar?"

"Yes, boss. He came in a little while ago. When you called me into your office, Tarzan took over behind the bar."

"Go relieve him, and tell him I want to see him right now."

"Okay, boss." Pissclam left Red's office, and a minute or two later, Tarzan sat down in the seat in front of Red's desk. "You wanted to see me, Red?" Red handed a note to Tarzan that had a phone number written on it, and he handed it to Tarzan.

"Yes. Call Fred Thompson at the Islip Executive Airport and tell him I want to discuss the price of renting his Lear Jet for a long-range flight out of the country for a week or two. Tell him I want to discuss this in private in my office as soon as he can get here. Make the call now, Tarzan. Tell him it's important, and I'd like to see him as soon as possible." Tarzan left the office and used the phone in the conference room and made the call. A few minutes later, he was back in Red's office. "Fred said to tell you he'd cancel all of his appointments and he'll see you first thing in the morning. He wants to avoid the early morning rush hour traffic on the Long Island Expressway, so he'll try to be here between ten and eleven tomorrow morning."

Red lived upstairs, and he always made it a habit to rise early. He went through his usual routine of showering and shaving. Then he went to his closet door and took one of several two-thousand-dollar suits hanging neatly on hooks in his closet. Today, he chose a navy blue suit, a four-hundred-fifty-dollar Stefano Ricci silk shirt, a fifty-dollar Italian silk tie, Bally of Switzerland (not Italy) shoes, and gold Tiffany cufflinks. When Red walked downstairs to his office, he looked as if he stepped off the cover of *Vogue* magazine.

Fred Thompson walked into the club at ten forty-five and, having spotted Red seated at his favorite table, he headed there. There were times Red used Fred's services, but it wasn't often, because Red rarely left the country or the comforts of the Starlight Club, but he had used Thompson's services in the past.

The Sicilian Caper

Red had become comfortable with the man, and he felt he could trust the affable pilot, but only to a point, and never with family business. "Do you need both a plane and a pilot, or if I remember correctly, you have your own pilot you could use. Which is it, Red?"

"I have a pilot I've used before. He's an ex-combat pilot and I'll use him, so I'll only need a plane. Do you have a suitable business jet I could rent for a week or two?"

Thompson absently ran his hand through his hair. "We're currently servicing a Lockheed Jetstar L-329 capable of flying internationally, and I haven't scheduled the plane to be placed in service for four weeks. I know you're in a hurry, and even though I've been working my crew hard the past two weeks, getting my grounded aircraft placed back into service, I can have the Jetstar's service completed and inspected and ready for you to use in two or three days. With that being said, I need to qualify it by saying that it depends on whether the workforce is available to work overtime." Red was about to say something, but Thompson waved it away. "Don't worry, it'll be ready to fly when you need it. Just give me the date and time you'll be needing it."

"Before I can leave, I need a week to put my affairs in order. Let's set the date for a week from today. I'll call you the day after tomorrow to give you the information you need about my licensed pilot, the guy who is qualified to fly this plane to Europe." Red purposely left the destination vague because he preferred to keep his plans to himself. Fred couldn't talk to anyone about things he knew nothing of. Red was a believer in Carlo Gambino's manner of communicating with members of his mob. He just nodded, or he shook his head, or he would just wave his hand to press a point. He was as silent as a man could be when communicating with someone, even if it was in his own house. His philosophy in his home was "they tapped our phones, and they wired our house." If he was in his club or at someone else's house, his philosophy remained the same. He never said much, because they tapped the phones and they wired everyone's home. Wherever the boss of bosses was at the moment, they tapped the phones and they wired the place, which was why Red had the Starlight Club and the upstairs apartments swept for bugs every other day, and he made sure his men checked anyone who claimed to be from the telephone company, Con-Edison power company, or the water company, or from any city agency. One of his men always accompanied anyone who provided a reason they had to inspect the Starlight Club, or the apartments on the upper floor.

Red preferred the Lockheed Jetstar, because it seated eight to ten people, in addition to two crew members, plus the Lockheed Jetstar would fly him non-stop to the Punta Raisi airport just nineteen miles northwest of Palermo, the capital city of Sicily. He dialed Fred Thompson's number. "I'll be flying out on Sunday morning, Fred. Will the plane be ready?"

"It's ready now, Red. So whenever you decide to leave, give me a phone call and I'll have the plane ready. I'll need your pilot's credentials, and a copy of the insurance policy you have on the plane."

"I'll send one of my men to you tomorrow with the items you need. This way, we can take off as soon as we get there without wasting time."

"It's a good idea to send one of your men with the info I need, Red. Getting that information will eliminate a lot of wasted time beforehand."

"The man I'm sending with the information you asked me for is Pissclam. He'll be at your office to see you sometime this afternoon with a check for the rental price of the jet for one week. If we use the jet longer, I'll pay what I owe you when we get back. Now that we've concluded our business, I'd like you to call me back from a payphone at this number in a half hour. It's important, so I'll expect a call from you in thirty minutes." Red told him he'd use the pay phone in the mechanics' shack across the street, and then he hung up. Then he dialed another of his men, Captain Frankie, his pilot.

Frankie was a fighter pilot during his tour of duty while in the Korean war. When Red decided to fly to Sicily to settle the squatter problem Tarzan had for the house he inherited from his father, Red asked Larry Epstein the president of Columbia pictures if he could borrow his jet aircraft. Epstein agreed, but Captain Frankie flew the jet. For this flight, Red called Captain

The Sicilian Caper

Frankie, and careful not to talk freely on the phone, he told him to drop everything he was doing and stop by the Starlight Club as soon as he could because he wanted to discuss a trip he was planning with him as his pilot. "Do you remember the last plane you piloted when me and a few of our friends took our vacation in Italy?"

"I remember that trip very well. You're talking about the plane you borrowed from your Hollywood friend in Southern California, right?"

"That's right. Well, I'm planning another vacation and I want you to pilot the plane. You'll be flying me and a few friends to Europe. The plane you'll be piloting is a Lockheed Jetstar L-329 jet I rented for seven days. I'll fill you in on where we're flying to, and other details when you get here." Red would tell him specifically which country he'd be flying to when he got to the Starlight Club. He could speak candidly with Frankie in the conference room without having to beat around the bush, and without the fear that someone could be listening in on their conversation. Red hung up the phone and walked across the street to the parking lot. For the convenience of the customers, the payphone was located outside and to the right side of the office in plain sight. Just as Red checked his watch, the phone rang. Red picked up the phone. "Red here."

"Red, it's Fred. What did you want to tell me?"

"Fred, I need a favor. I would have discussed it with you when you were here, but it slipped my mind. You had left about a half hour when I remembered what I wanted to ask you."

"What's the favor you want from me, Red?"

"I need you to modify something in the plane for me. It's worth a grand if you do it for me."

"Go ahead, I'm listening." Red was a little uneasy telling Fred what he wanted him to do on the phone. He felt naked, but he had no choice. He had to tell Fred what he needed from him, so he blurted it out. "Fred, I want you to build a hidden compartment somewhere on the plane. The last plane I used, the owner had a secret compartment built seamlessly into the cargo area. I won't be carrying illegal drugs or illegal goods. I need a place to hide a few pieces of hardware. I'm not going to go into detail about it, but I'll be visiting some very dangerous men, and I want to feel the comfort of something substantial in my pocket, and I'm not talking about my pecker. Do you understand what I'm telling you?"

"Yes, I understand."

"Can you do this favor for me?"

"Not for a grand, I can't. But I'll consider doing it for five grand."

Red's temper flared for a moment, but he got it back under control. "What do you mean you'll consider it? Either you'll do it or you won't. Spill it out plainly."

"I'll do it for five grand."

Red could have bartered the price down a grand or two, but he wasn't in the mood to haggle. "All right. You have a deal. Get it done by the time I pick up the plane."

"I want to be paid in cash."

Fred was talking Red's language now. He understood cash. "I'll give you the cash when I pick up the plane. Just make sure you do a good job, because international customs inspectors will check the plane carefully when we land."

The Sicilian Caper

CHAPTER 10

Captain Frankie sat in Red's office listening to Red explain where they were flying to and what the mission consisted of. Frankie listened carefully. Red explained how they discovered there was an informer working in one crew. He told Frankie about Enzo Batto and how he had discovered that Batto was behind the robberies they were experiencing. "Knowing that Batto was behind the robberies, I was told that as soon as they split the money from each robbery, Batto quickly flew back to Sicily and disappeared. I'm flying to Sicily to see if I can pick up a lead and discover where he's hiding out. I plan to meet with a Sicilian cop I know and talk to him, and then I intend to meet with the local mafia leader. I know the man's name is Don Castillo. The Don may have fresh information on Batto's whereabouts for me. I just hope that Batto isn't a part of Castillo's mob. If he is, then that could present a formidable problem for us."

When Red finished, Frankie asked him. "How many men will come with us, Red?"

"I'm taking Trenchie, Tarzan, Joey Boy, Tic-Tok, Sal, Ron, and Pissclam. Questions, Frankie?"

"No, Red, but I like the L-329. It's a new aircraft, and it's a good ship to fly. I flew the military version of the jet, and it impressed me. It'll take you anywhere in the world in comfort. Your movie businesses are picking up and your Las Vegas casinos are doing a brisk business, so look into buying one for your personal use." Frankie's suggestion to buy a long-range aircraft made sense. Especially convincing were the points he made about Red's Hollywood money machines, his two movie studios, and then he thought of his very profitable Las Vegas casinos, his Lake Topaz casino, his Anaheim Card club, and his other various legitimate businesses. Although he had given little thought to owning an executive jet aircraft. He could afford to buy the aircraft, as money wasn't a problem for him. Owning a plane was a novel idea, and something he would give considerable thought to. But it would have to wait until he tracked down and took care of Enzo. Once he took this pain in the ass murdering thug Enzo out of the equation, and he was no longer a thorn in his side, he just might treat himself to a long-range business jet.

The next morning, two things happened. Red's jet landed at the Punta Raisi airport, and the two men Don Castillo assigned to protect Enzo arrived at Mario's tobacco shop in Gratteri, telling him Don Castillo sent them to protect Enzo Batto, and they were ready for duty. Enzo had been talking to a local man he knew from his past, and when he heard the two men tell Mario Don Castillo sent them, he excused himself and he stepped forward. "I am Enzo Batto. What are your names?"

"My name is Giuseppi, and my partner's name is Tomasso." When the person Enzo had been talking to heard the man say Don Castillo sent him, he quickly dropped a few coins on the counter, picked up his two cigars, shoved them in his pocket, and immediately left the tobacco shop. He wanted nothing to do with the men and what they were saying. But it relieved Enzo that Don Castillo had kept his word and sent him the two men.

"I am happy to meet you men. Your jobs are two-fold. Tomasso, your job is to remain here and be wary of strangers. I want you to observe and then follow any strangers who loiter in the town, or make inquiries about me. If you see anyone suspicious, tell Mario to take you to the cave I use as a hideout. Once you know where my hideout is, you can come directly there, Tomasso. You!" he said, pointing to the second man. "You will come with me, Giuseppi. You will be my eyes and ears. You are here to protect me from those that I'm certain will come for me."

Giuseppi nodded, and he asked, "Do you want me to take my *doppietta* with me wherever we go?"

Enzo was silent for a moment, and then he acknowledged the question. "I think it is necessary for you to carry your

The Sicilian Caper

shotgun with you during these troubled times. This way, wherever we go, we will have the protection of the *doppietta* you carry with you at all times. It is a powerful weapon for you to have, and it will prove useful if we run into trouble. Just make sure to load up your gun belt with shotgun shells."

Giuseppi's eyes narrowed, and his face took on a grim look as his hand slid down to his side and he pulled his vest to the side, revealing a holstered gun. "It's a World War II forty-five automatic. I took it off the body of a dead officer and I feel naked without it. I always carry my *pistola* with me wherever I go."

"Take your automatic with you too. We don't want you to feel naked now, do we?" Enzo said lightly.

"What about me?" Tomasso asked. "Do you want me to be armed too?"

"Of course I want you armed. You're no good to me if you can't defend me... that's the reason you are here... you are here to keep me safe and protect me from my enemies. That is it... plain and simple, just do as I say and watch my back, and keep an eye out for strangers, and we will get along."

While the plane was being searched by Italian customs inspectors, Red scanned the terminal for a payphone but didn't see any. A customs inspector noticed Red looking around the hangar, searching for something, and he guessed he was looking for the payphone, which happened often in that hangar. "Pardon me, signore, but I notice you looking for something. Possibly a payphone?"

"Yes, I told a friend that I would call him the moment I landed in Sicily."

"Go through the door leading into the terminal, and as you walk in, you'll see a payphone on the wall on your right."

"Thank you for your help, Inspector. I would never have found the payphone without your help." Red said to the inspector as he excused himself to make his phone call.

"Hello. Is this Captain John Scatore?" Red asked when the phone was picked up.

"Yes, this is Captain Scatore. I recognize your voice, Red. I hope you called me to ask me and my wife to have dinner with you and your beautiful wife."

"I'm sorry to tell you I couldn't take my wife with me on this trip. I'm here for a few days on business, John. Your kind of business. I had hoped we could meet for dinner alone, because I have a problem I believe you may help me with."

"Hmm, I see. Where are you now, Red?"

"We just landed at the landed at the Punta Raisi airport in the Madoni section of Sicily. Right now, I'm in the town of Gratteri."

"What are you doing in Gratteri Red? Gratteri is a tiny little town at the base of a mountain, and there's nothing to do there."

"I know all of what you're telling me, but there's someone I'm looking forward to meeting, and he's staying there."

"Oh!" Captain Scatore uttered, as recognition of what Red may be doing in Gratteri dawned on him. "Red, do nothing rash, at least until we talk and you tell me what's going on. Please promise me you'll talk to me first before doing anything you may regret."

Red chuckled. "Okay, Mother. I'll wait 'til we have our little talk. If you prefer, I can send our jet to pick you up. Just tell me where to send the plane."

"There's no need for that, Red. I'm tied up working on a case for the next few days. But I will be free, and at your disposal this weekend."

"What if I flew into Palermo? Could you meet me at the airport after you get off work? I have a few questions I must ask you that can't wait until the weekend."

Scatore's law enforcement senses were on full alert. He understood now what his earlier feelings about Red flying into Sicily unannounced were telling him. Red was on the hunt and he needed information he could get from no one but him. "All right. Meeting you at the Palermo Airport, as you suggested, would work for me."

"What time would be good for you?" Red asked.

"Let's talk over dinner. Is seven tonight good for you?" Scatore asked.

"Seven o'clock is perfect."

"I'll charter a helicopter to take me to the Palermo airport."

"Good. I'll meet you at the helipad and we'll take my car to

The Sicilian Caper

the Bellotero Ristorante. It's near the airport and it serves good food. We can talk there."

"I'll call you back after I've reserved a helicopter and let you know what time I'll be landing there."

Ten minutes later, Red called Captain Scatore and told him he reserved a chopper flight and the pilot assured him they would land at Palermo airport at seven. With that done, Red walked back into the hangar where his men were milling around the jet. He approached Tarzan and asked him if the weapons were off the plane. "Follow me back into the plane, Red."

Red said nothing and followed Tarzan onto the plane where they sat down opposite one another in plush leather seats. The only lights in the plane was light from the hangar filtering through the jet's windows. The interior of the jet was dimly lit, which was the way Tarzan wanted it. "Was the plane inspected by the customs agents?"

"Yeah, the customs inspectors went through the plane, giving it a thorough search, but it satisfied both inspectors that everything was as it should be, and they left."

Red, hearing Tarzan's news, sat back in his comfortable seat and relaxed. "Just hearing we satisfied the inspectors is a load off of my mind. How about the weapons? Did you take all the weapons off the plane?"

"Look out the window and look at the men, Red. Do you see them?"

"Yeah. So?"

"Look at the suitcases on the cart beside them. See them?"

"Yeah, I see them."

"The weapons are in the suitcases on that cart."

"Where are our suitcases with our clothes and personal items?"

"I had that luggage put in the car we rented. I didn't want anyone getting suspicious of us having so much luggage, so I put them in the car to get them out of the way of nosy airport workers."

"Good idea, Tarzan. What's the holdup with this luggage?"

"There's no holdup, Red. I sent Pissclam to get the second car I rented. He should be here any minute. When he gets here with the car, I'll have the men wheel the luggage to the second car and stack them in it."

As Tarzan was explaining what was unfolding to Red, Pissclam pulled up with the second car. The men, eager to get the luggage into the car and away from a curious inspector, wheeled the luggage to Pissclam, and Tic-Tok, who were waiting to stack the heavy luggage into the car.

CHAPTER 11

The chopper set down at 6:55 pm, and Captain Scatore was there waiting for Red. Red was glad to see his friend for several reasons. One was he did not know the area, nor where to find the restaurant Scatore mentioned while on the phone. Red stepped out of the chopper and embraced his friend. "It's good to see you, John."

"Same here, Red. Come, I have my car parked outside the terminal near the exit. It's a short drive, and the restaurant isn't far. Come, let's hurry to the car. I'm so hungry I could eat a bear."

The ride took a few minutes longer than usual because of heavy traffic, but the men were soon seated at a table and enjoying a drink. "Now tell me why you came to Sicily. No! Don't tell me. Let me guess. You are after someone and you came here to find him. Don't deny it; just tell me why you want him, and tell me what he did to you to make you come all the way to Sicily from America."

"I'm impressed, John. You are a very perceptive man, and you're on the right track, so I'll level with you, and even though you're a law men, you deserve to know the whole story, so I'll tell you everything right from the beginning." Red told Scatore how Enzo Batto killed his father and then he told his story until the events led to the present, leaving out of his story anything of a criminal nature, anything that would incriminate him. He would never tell an officer of the law, no matter what country that lawman worked for, anything that alluded to his criminal activities back in Queens. He ended the story by telling Scatore that he intended to visit Don Castillo to tell him why he came to Sicily, and then ask him if he knew where Enzo Batto was hiding.

Captain Scatore's brow furrowed. He wasn't happy with the idea of Red meeting with Don Castillo. The Don was a ruthless mafioso, and Scatore was afraid that if Red met with Don Castillo, he might not leave the meeting alive. "Look, my friend. I don't question you about what you do when you are in Queens, New York, but here in Sicily, you must follow the rules, because friend or no friend, I will not stand by and watch a bloodbath take place in my town."

"I made a mistake calling you, John. I thought you were a friend I could talk to honestly. Someone who could advise me on certain problems as only someone in law enforcement could. But it appears I was wrong." Red stood and was about to leave, but Scatore took his arm and asked him to sit down again.

"Let's talk, Red. Let's see if we can come up with a plan that won't get you killed."

Red sat back down, but couldn't imagine where this conversation would go. He was the head of a major Queens crime family, and Captain Scatore was an honest Sicilian police officer.

"Let me get something straight with you before we have our discussion. First off, I will not stand by and watch two factions shoot one another into oblivion. What I will do is advise you and I will answer questions you may have about Don Castillo. Now let's talk. How can I help you?"

"I want you to believe me. I'm not here to start a small war. All I want is to find Enzo Batto. Do you know him?"

Captain Scatore narrowed his eyes, his lips were slits, and Red could tell he wasn't comfortable answering his question. "Yes, I know him. He's been seen in the mountains somewhere near Gratteri."

Finally, something solid, Red thought. "So you think he's in the Gratteri region?" Red said.

"I didn't say that. I said we have seen him in that region of Sicily. If you want my opinion, I'd say there's a good chance that's where his hideout is."

"What makes you say that, John?"

"Enzo's cousin Mario has a tobacco shop in Gratteri, so I believe he would remain close to a relative where he could get

The Sicilian Caper

aid and support. But there is something you should know. One of my informers told me that Don Castelli sent two of his men to act as his bodyguards."

"So you're telling me the Don did him a favor? Why would he do that?"

"We know Enzo has plenty of money, and he spends it wisely, and that's why Don Castillo sent him two men. Enzo has to pay the men, so that means that the Don will get a cut of the money Enzo pays the men. The Don does nothing for nothing, unless he benefits from it."

"Thank you, John. What you just told me about the Don, and Enzo, was invaluable to me. I would wager a guess that no one other than you could have known the little known things you just told me about Don Castillo and Enzo Batto, and when I get back to New York, I'll show you how Big Red returns a favor."

Red checked the time on his gold Rolex. "I better get going. I have a helicopter waiting for me at the airport."

When they left the restaurant and were walking to the car, Scatore grabbed Red's arm and pulled him close. "Red, do nothing that will put me in a position where I'll have to arrest you. Promise me."

"I promise you I won't start anything, but if me or my men's lives are at risk, we will do everything in our power to protect ourselves, and if it means killing some people, then so be it. But I won't be the one to start trouble; I'll be the one to finish it. I know the position I've placed you in and I apologize for having to do that, but Enzo must be stopped before he kills more people. If it is at all possible, John, I'll try to bring you in at the finale."

"I would appreciate you bringing me in on this, Red. Look, play this by ear and keep in touch with me. If you do that, then I will do everything in my power to protect you. But only if you keep me in the loop."

"I'll do that, John. I promise."

Before Red was about to walk to the helicopter, he asked the captain, "Look John. I had planned on having one of my special nights, and no matter how this problem with Enzo works out, I'd like to repay you for the help you are giving me by inviting you to an all-expenses-paid vacation to join me at the Starlight Club for a special evening of entertainment and excellent cuisine."

"All expenses paid, you say?"

"Yes, even the airfare. I'll put you and your wife up in a guest room at the Starlight Club. You'll love it, and I'll show you and your wife the town."

"You mean New York City?"

"Yes, especially New York City."

"That's most generous of you, Red. I can't say that I'm not looking forward to accepting your generous offer, because I am. I've always wanted to visit New York City. If we take you up on your offer, could we go to the Copacabana nightclub? I've heard so much about it, that I promised myself that if I ever visited New York, I'd see a show at the famous Copacabana, and is the famous showman Billy Rose still doing his shows at... what's the name of the beach?"

"The name of the beach is Jones Beach, but no. He's doing his show at the Aquacade in Queens, and the shows are as popular as they have ever been."

"Do they still permit swimming at the Aquacade during the day?"

"Yes, and if you and your wife go to the Aquacade when you're in New York, it will be a very enjoyable day for both of you. And after a day of swimming in the sun, you and your wife will freshen up and change clothes at the Starlight Club. We'll have dinner and then we'll take in a Billy Rose aqua show at the Aquacade."

The pilot waved to get Red's attention. When Red turned to him, the pilot gestured, pointing to his watch.

Red got the message, and he excused himself. "The chopper's waiting, John. I have to go now, but I'll be in touch with you soon, and we'll arrange you and your wife's trip to New York as my guest."

As soon as Red got into the waiting chopper, it lifted off for the short flight to Punta Raisi airport. Tarzan had been waiting at the heliport for Red to get back from his dinner engagement with the police captain. The other men went straight to the historic Hotel Villa Politi. They had a few drinks while waiting

The Sicilian Caper

for Red to return from his dinner engagement.

Immediately after Red and Tarzan entered the hotel, Red told Tarzan, "Find the men and tell them to meet me here in the lounge. I want to discuss our plans in private, and the lounge is as private as we'll find."

Tarzan called the room to tell the men that Red wanted to meet with them, and shortly after, the men met for drinks in a quiet corner of the lounge. "What did you find out, Red?" Tarzan asked.

"The good news is Enzo is in a little town in Sicily, Gratteri. His cousin owns the tobacco store in town. I think if we let ourselves into the tobacco shop and surprised Enzo's cousin Mario, we might convince his cousin to tell us where Enzo is staying," He said it tongue in cheek because everyone talks when tortured properly, and Red and his men knew the correct procedures on how to inflict torture.

"What else did you find out, boss?" Pissclam asked.

"Enzo has two bodyguards. They're a part of Don Castillo's mob. Castillo is the local mafia chieftain, and he's a greedy prick. He gets a piece of every rotten deal in his region. He ordered Enzo to pay his men for protecting him and he gets a third of whatever Enzo pays them, which in this case is $300.00 a week each, and the Don gets a third of that."

Trenchie, who had been quiet up until now, asked Red, "So the local Don assigned two men to protect Enzo. How do you think he'll use them?"

Red gave a sly grin. "I know how I would use them, but I'd like to hear how you would use them, Trenchie?"

"It's just common sense, Red. I wouldn't have two men doing the same job. I'd split them up. I'd have one hang around the store keeping his eye out for strangers, and I'd have the other man stay as close to me as stink on shit."

Red laughed and slapped Trenchie on his back. "Good thinking, Trenchie, 'cause that's exactly what I would do. Now remember that the two men sent by Castillo are professional killers. They made their bones a long time ago, so a little bloodshed won't bother them at all. Now here's the rub. If we kill one, or both of them, we'll have the Don and all of his men looking to kill us. If we only take out one of his men, he's still going to be pissed off."

"Fuck him and his fat ass being pissed off," Trenchie said. "Let the bastard come, and I'll take care of him. I'll rip him apart personally."

"Remember, guys. This ain't Queens. We're in Sicily, the land of the vendetta. Now I feel as Trenchie does. No man scares us, because we hold the power of life and death in our two hands, but we're going to be extra careful on how we handle this job. I don't want it getting away from us, but if the shit hits the fan, then so be it. We'll take them on one at a time or all at once if it comes down to it." Red looked around at the guys. "I never saw the secret compartment they built for us, so when we get back to the plane, I want somebody to show it to me. I'd like to know what weapons we took with us on the plane? Tarzan, give me a weapons run-down. What did we take with us?"

The Sicilian Caper

CHAPTER 12

The following day, Red and his men drove to Gratteri and parked on a side street before entering the town proper. "Tarzan, you're elected. Take a walk through town. Look for the tobacco shop, but try not to get too close to it. We have to assume one man is watching for strangers. If he spots you, he will warn Enzo that a stranger has showed up in town. If he does that, Enzo will bolt and we may never find him again. So be careful. You speak the Sicilian language like a native, so speak Sicilian and not English. Don't let anyone know you're an American. If they question you, tell them about your father's house and you're here to meet a girl, or just use your imagination and tell them anything to put them at ease so they'll relax and won't suspect a stranger."

They put their plan to work on the following evening. They'd enter the shop when the town was asleep, and remain there until morning when the shop's owner showed up for work. Red assigned Tic-Tok to jimmy a window in the store's rear and enter the tobacco shop, and once the window was open, the rest of the men would follow. Once inside, they'd wait for Enzo's cousin to show up for work. It would involve all but one man in the break-in. Trenchie was told to protect their rear. Red didn't want any surprises, so he assigned Trenchie to remain in his car to protect their flank and to make sure everything went as planned.

It was well after midnight when they put their plan to work. The sleepy little town, with all the lights blanketed by the darkness of night, was practically invisible. The men were all armed with the military version of Colt's automatic 1911A1's they had taken from a warehouse in Maspeth, Queens a few months back and stored in their warehouse.

Trenchie watched the men use the darkness to hide in shadows as they approached the rear of the tobacco shop. Tic-Tok jimmied the window, and when he slid it open, he stepped through the window. He offered his hand to Pissclam to help steady him as he, too, stepped through the window. Trenchie watched the scene unfold until sudden unexpected gunfire lit up the interior of the small tobacco shop. They riddled Tic-Tok with bullets, and he fell dead to the floor. They shot Joey Boy in several places, but he got off a few shots, hitting the man who shot Tic-Tok, and the force of the forty-five slugs hitting the man in the center of his chest jerked him off of his feet and he flew backwards, slamming him into the wall opposite the window they entered the store through.

Tarzan dragged Joey Boy to the window and handed him to Red, who pulled him free of the window. Tarzan knew they shot Joey Boy two or three times, but he couldn't tell how badly they'd hurt him. They'd have to wait until they could get him to a place of safety. Tarzan climbed out of the window and picked up Joey Boy as if he was a feather. He used the fireman's carry to carry Joey Boy through the back alley away from the tobacco shop. The men were as quiet as church mice as they made their way along the back alley, when suddenly, the rear door of a house they were passing opened. The men spun around to face the danger with their guns drawn, pointing at the source of danger. It surprised them to see an attractive young woman who appeared to be in her early to mid-twenties step out onto the porch and wave for the men to come into her home. "Quickly," she ordered in Sicilian-accented English. "Come into my house before they see you. Hurry, they'll be here shortly, and they can see you, so be quick, please. I don't want them to see which house you entered. They would kill me if they knew I helped you." The men carried Joey Boy into the young lady's home with her leading the way. She led the men carrying Joey Boy into her bedroom and told them to put him on her bed.

"Are you sure? Because if this is a setup, you'll regret it." Red said and then told his men to keep their guns on her.

She shrugged as if it were of no concern. "Your friend needs

The Sicilian Caper

the bed more than I do. I can sleep on the couch, and I can tend to him better here in my bedroom." When she settled Joey Boy comfortably in her bed, she led Red and the men to her living room. "I'll put the coffee on, but you will have to watch it. While the coffee is percolating, I will see if the bullets are still in your friend." She went back to Joey Boy, and she gave him a thorough examination. Red watched her light a match and sterilize a needle, and then he watched her thread the needle. "Please hand me the bottle of alcohol on the bureau. I'll need one of you to hold him down while I pour the alcohol into the entrance and exit wound, and then I'll have to stitch the wounds closed. He was lucky, because two bullets went clean through him without hitting a major organ. The third bullet is still in him. I'll have to dig it out, so you'll have to make sure he doesn't move."

Joey Boy's eyes opened, and he spoke in a low whisper. "Don't worry, beautiful, I won't be a problem. Just get these slugs out of me." Then his eyes closed, and he slipped into a deep, blissful unconsciousness.

Red didn't ask her questions. Questions could wait. All he wanted was for Joey Boy to survive the night, and then hope that he got better. The men gathered around the woman as she stitched Joey Boy's entrance and exit bullet wounds closed. With that done, she looked up at Red, who she by now knew was the man in charge. "That was the easy part. Now comes the hard part, and that is why I need you to hold him down so he doesn't move. Please hand me the bullet probe instrument. It's that long metal object on the night table. If he moves while I have the probe inside of him, it could move and rupture a vital organ, or a major artery, so please hold him tight. Even though he appears to be asleep, the pain could make him jump involuntarily. Hold him so he cannot move while I have the probe inside of him. Understand?" she said, looking at the men surrounding her bed. They all nodded in agreement. She sighed and picked up the probe and carefully inserted it into the third bullet hole. "I feel the bullet," she said excitedly to the men, pleased that she had located the bullet. "Now to get it out." She picked up her bullet-extractor and carefully used it to remove the bullet. Pointing to the bureau, she asked Tarzan to hand her the bottle of alcohol, which she poured liberally into the bullet's entrance wound. She stitched the wound closed and finished bandaging Joey Boy and left him sleeping.

"Take a seat at the table. I'll bring the coffee."

Red smiled, thinking of how efficient this young woman was. She had just sewed two of Joey's bullet holes closed, and pulled a bullet out of a third bullet hole, and now, as if nothing untoward had happened, she was serving coffee to a bunch of strange men.

The young woman brought the tray with the coffee pot and cups, and she poured each of the men a cup of coffee. "I'm Red and these men are my friends. That big guy there is Trenchie." Trenchie raised his hand in acknowledgement. "That's Tarzan. He owns a house in Sicily. And that fellow is Sammy, but everyone calls him Pissclam. The fellow using your bed is Joey Boy, that man is Sal, and the fellow with the dashing mustache is Ronny. There is one other man, our pilot. His name is Frankie, and you'll meet him soon. Now that you know our names, how about you telling us yours?"

"My name is Sophia," she told them with a thick Sicilian accent. "I studied medicine at the university, and I had to learn a second language, which was English, and that's how I learned to speak English."

"Did you get your medical degree?" Red asked.

"No. My mother was already dead when my father died. All he left me was this house, but no money to continue my education. I had no money of my own to continue college, so now I teach school."

"Why did you help us? You know what will happen to you if they discover you helped us. So why did you do it?"

"I am twenty-three years old now, but when I was nineteen, I was engaged to a wonderful young man, but he did a stupid thing. He borrowed money from Don Castillo to start a business, a little shoe store, but he was late with his payment to Don Castillo, so Castillo had his goons beat my fiancé almost to death, and they took all his stock as interest on his loan. They left him penniless and badly injured, almost near death. I took him in and tried to nurse him back to health, but he was seriously injured internally, and he died three days later. I went to the authorities, but they did nothing because everyone involved had an alibi. But they always turn a blind eye with Don Castillo. All the guilty men were elsewhere at the time the beating took place. I hated Don Castillo, and I longed for the day when I could hurt him. Maybe helping you tonight was a way of me hurting him. So tonight when I heard gun-fire, I watched, and I waited, and sure enough, I watched you men carrying your friend and I knew they shot him. I wanted to help you, not only to hurt Don Castillo, but even though I didn't know the wounded man, I wanted to help him and maybe save his life."

Red smiled. "Well, you certainly did that. You saved his life."

"I think so, but it is too soon to say that I saved his life. If he makes it through the night, that would be an encouraging sign, and I think he'd be past the crisis and he'd live."

"Don't worry, Sophia, I witnessed enough gunshot wounds to recognize a man who, if given proper care, which Joey Boy is getting, and enough time to heal, he will recover." Red sipped his coffee and then he asked Sophia a question. "If you had the money, would you go back to college and get your medical degree?"

She thought about Red's question for a few moments before answering him. "Yes. I believe I would go back and finish medical college and get my medical degree. Why do you ask?"

"When we finish our business in Sicily, we'll discuss how to pay for your college expenses. Because that's what I intend to do. Pay all your expenses so you can get your medical degree."

What Red told her shocked Sophia. "But... why would you want to pay for my education?"

"I saw how you took care of Joey Boy. You knew what you were doing and you're not even a doctor yet. You saved my friend and I want to repay you for doing that. Put your mind at ease, Sophia. All of your problems are about to go away, but first we have to repay the people that did this to Joey Boy." Sophia looked at Red with a confused expression on her face. "Why are you looking so confused, Sophia? Did I say something you may not have understood?"

"No, Mr.... I forgot your name. Mr.?"

"All my friends call me Red. I want you to call me Red too."

"Aren't you afraid of those men, Red? I certainly am."

"And yet you took a chance and invited us into your home, and then you saved Joey Boy. That sounds pretty courageous to me, but to answer your question, Sophia, no... I'm not afraid of those men. It is they who should be afraid of me. Let me ask you a few questions, Sophia. Can you walk past any of those men and not be afraid they might cause you harm?"

"No. I'm afraid of them, and I always try to avoid them if possible. In fact, I hardly leave my home to shop. I have my neighbor shop for me because I'm afraid I might run into one or more of them."

"Well, that is about to change. I would feel much more comfortable knowing that when we leave Gratteri, you can leave your home and shop without the fear of being accosted by those lowlifes. I may have to return here a few times to make it happen, but that is what I intend to do. Make it safe for you and your neighbors to leave your homes without the fear of being harmed by those thugs."

CHAPTER 13

"I knew they would come. Now I have to go on the run again," Enzo said.

"No, you don't. They killed one man, and they shot a second man three times. He's probably dead by now. Didn't Don Castillo protect you? He likes you, and I think he'd like you to join his mob."

"You think so, Mario?"

"Think about it. Why would he send his men to protect you from the Americans?"

That was a question Enzo couldn't answer. Not now at least, but he'd discover the answer to that question soon enough. Maybe Mario was right. Maybe Don Castillo saw something in him. Something he could use, and the protection the Don could offer him, would neutralize the threat that Red represented. When things cooled down a bit, he would visit Don Castillo and find out if Mario was right. But for now, things were too hot to even leave the safety of his cave. No one knew of his secret hideout. No one until now, he thought. The mountain hid his cave so well, no one would ever find it, but he was so frightened of Red finding him, he had made a mistake, because now Giuseppi knew about his cave. He should never have told him to come with him to his hideout. That was a mistake he'd have to rectify if he wanted to live. Maybe he could kill Giuseppi and blame it on Red and his men. But if he did that, he'd have to kill Mario too. Mario was his cousin, but if push came to shove, he'd kill him too... and blame it on the mobster from Queens, New York. Enzo shook his head, hoping it wouldn't come to that. He liked Mario, and if he had a choice, he wouldn't hurt him, but if it was him or Enzo, then the choice was clear: he would kill him and have no regrets.

Enzo looked outside his cave, and saw Giuseppi watching, looking for a shrub that jostled when there was no wind, something, anything, a movement that shouldn't be there. Enzo shook his head again. This man was too valuable to kill. If an intruder found his hideout, he would be Enzo's first line of defense. No! He wouldn't do anything to Giuseppi, not now, but maybe when this was over.

The cave opening wasn't a hole in the mountain with a hollow inside of it. It was a vertical slit in the mountain's face, covered by thick brush. Looking at the cave's entrance from the front facing the mountain, no one would guess there was an opening that led into the mountain. Enzo had found the opening when he was a young boy tending his father's sheep. He used to let them wander up the slope to feed, and one day, he lost one of his sheep. Enzo went looking for him, but couldn't find him. Then he heard the little sheep call out to him, letting him know he was lost and frightened. Enzo followed the bleating sound until it led him to the opening. He couldn't believe how many times he had passed this opening without ever realizing it was there. If it wasn't for his little sheep getting lost, he would have never found it. He told no one about the cave; it was his little secret. But he explored every inch, because deep in his subconscious mind, without being aware of the significance of his discovery, he knew the cave was an important discovery, at least important to him. But now Giuseppi knew of it. Even Mario knew of his cave, but Enzo had allowed no one to enter it. Even Mario, Enzo's first cousin, wasn't invited into the cave, and now… Giuseppi knew of his cave. He knew where it was, and how to enter it. This would never do, Enzo thought. Enzo pushed that thought aside, because right now he had a greater problem. He knew Red would never give up. He somehow tracked him here to Gratteri. How he knew to find him here, he would never know, but he did. Now Big Red would have to be dealt with, and with Don Castillo's help together, they might neutralize the powerful New York mobster permanently. At least he hoped that was the case.

Joey Boy's eyes fluttered open. He was groggy, his mouth

The Sicilian Caper

dry as burnt toast. He turned his head slowly because it felt as if he was dragging an anchor. It surprised him to see Red and the boys sitting in chairs watching him. Then a slim figure glided in front of him. "So you're finally awake. How do you feel?"

Joey Boy's tongue wouldn't work for a moment and he couldn't speak. But finally, he said a few words. "I feel as though a truck ran over me." Then, with difficulty, he looked up, and he shook his head. "They... finally got... me. I... must... have died... because... an angel... is standing near... me, and, and... she's asking me... how I feel."

Trenchie grunted, "He's all right. If he sees an angel, he's getting better. Tomorrow, he'll be chasing her around the bed." The boys laughed quietly, relieved that Joey Boy would pull through.

"Okay," Red said. "Let's step into the living room. I want to discuss how we pay these bastards back for what they did to Tic-Tok and Joey Boy."

The men sat in the living room, but were silent as Sophia brought them coffee and a plate of pastries. "Sorry, this is all I can offer you for now. Tomorrow, I will ask Rosa—she's my neighbor—to do me a favor and buy me groceries from the store."

That raised a red flag for Red. "Be careful not to order more food than usual. You don't want the person ringing up your food to get suspicious."

"Red's right, Sophia, be careful not to make anyone suspicious because you're buying more than enough food for one person," Tarzan said.

"Where is the nearest payphone that I can use?"

"The nearest payphone is in front of Mario's tobacco store. There is another payphone near the blacksmith's shop, but it is three blocks from here."

Red thought about it for a minute and then he spoke to Sophia. "Sophia, you told us you were engaged to a young man."

"Yes. So?"

"What I was curious about, did he leave any of his clothing here?"

"I still have his jacket and cap. It was all I had of his, and I just couldn't throw them away, or give them away."

"Can you get them for me, please?"

"Yes. I'll get them. I won't be but a minute."

Sophia returned with a black pea coat which looked like a coat worn by dock workers or those working in the shipyards. The cap was black and matched the jacket. "Perfect," Red said, turning to Tarzan. "Try the jacket and cap on, Tarzan. Let's see how it looks."

Tarzan put on the pea coat and cap, and they fit him perfect. "Now what, Red?"

"Now you're going to take a walk a few blocks to the payphone at the blacksmith's shop."

"Wait a minute, Red. How the hell am I going to find the place when I've never been in this town?"

"You'll never find it by yourself. I'll walk with you and take you to the payphone by the blacksmith's shop," Sophia said.

Red knew there was no other choice. "All right, you convinced me. You two will walk to the blacksmith's shop together. Excuse me a minute, I have to get something." Red walked into the privacy of the bedroom, and he took out his Colt automatic and screwed on the silencer he brought with him. If he ran into trouble, he intended to end the trouble silently. He handed the gun with the silencer attached to Tarzan.

"Okay Sophia, now that I have this equalizer with me, I'm all set. The payphone is waiting, so let's go for our walk."

Red handed Tarzan a slip of paper with the Islip air terminal's number on it. "Call Captain Frankie and ask him to make an international call to Fred Thompson at Islip Executive Airport. Tell him we're tied up and won't be back for another two weeks. We'll pay him for the extra time when we get back. Oh, and tell him to find another jet just like the one we rented from him. Ask him if this one is for sale. If it is, tell him not to interest anyone else in it. Ask him if he'll apply the cost for the extra days we're using the jet to the purchase price. If he'll do that, then I'll buy the plane." After giving Tarzan his instructions, he thought to himself, *If I'm going to pay a fortune by renting the damn plane, I might as well own it.*

Tarzan looked like a native Sicilian dock worker walking

The Sicilian Caper

alongside Sophia wearing his newly gained navy blue pea coat and cap. He made the phone call to Islip's Executive Airport and was glad that Fred Thompson was there to pick up the phone. He told him all that Red asked him to and then he informed Thompson that they needed to use the jet for a few weeks longer. Tarzan asked him if the jet was for sale, would he apply the cost of using the jet for the extra days to the purchase price? Fred was a little strapped for cash and he surprised Tarzan by telling him he'd sell Red the jet, and he'd deduct the extra cost from the sale price. In order to solidify the deal, Red would have to overnight him a thirty-thousand-dollar goodwill check as a deposit. Plus Red must agree to hangar the plane at Islip Airport, and have Fred's company maintain the jet. "That should be no problem for Red," Tarzan told Thompson. After he hung up, he couldn't wait to get back to Sophia's house to give Red the good news.

Tarzan took Sophia by the arm and they walked away from the blacksmith's shop toward Sophia's home, when unexpectedly, a figure stepped out of an alley and fell in behind the walking couple. "Stop and don't turn around. Walk slowly back to the alley." Tarzan and Sophia complied and meekly walked into the dark alley, which was between an empty house on one side and a dimly lit house on the other side that appeared to have only one light on. Tarzan spoke to the man in a thick Sicilian accent, asking why they were being led into the alley. "What did we do?" he asked submissively. "What have we done to you, that you intend us harm?"

The man laughed. "Who said I was going to harm you? We're just taking a little walk, that's all we're doing. Now when we get into the alley, that's another story," he said, chuckling. Because Tarzan had his back to the man, and due to the darkness, the man couldn't see Tarzan put his hand into his pea coat's pocket and pull his gun. "Get up against the wall," the man ordered.

"Can we at least turn around and face you?" Tarzan asked.

"Yes. You can turn around and look at the man who is going to kill you. It's not something I enjoy doing, but orders are orders. You can understand that, can't you?"

Sophia was trembling with fright. She grabbed Tarzan's

arm, but he shoved her arm off and abruptly he pushed her away roughly. "Who ordered you to kill us?" Tarzan asked.

"I suppose there's no harm in granting the condemned man a last request. You ask who ordered me to kill you, well, it was Don Castillo. You came to Sicily uninvited, and you killed one of his men."

"Thank you. I appreciate you telling me that."

"You know, you are not a bad guy. It's too bad I have to kill you, but you understand, orders are orders."

"Yes. Orders are orders," Tarzan said, and with his hand still in his pocket, he raised the gun so it pointed directly at the assassin's chest and the automatic coughed twice. The gunshots hit the assassin twice in his chest, killing him instantly. Tarzan pulled the dead man's body into the shrubs behind the garage, but before leaving him, he frisked the body for identification. He found his wallet and quickly sifted through it, but found nothing of importance but a few hundred dollars, which he pocketed. He replaced the wallet, took his gun, and he dragged Sophia out of the alley, but just as they cleared the alley, Tarzan saw a shadow reflected on the wall of the empty house, and without thinking of who it might be, he shoved Sophia roughly to the ground as he spun around, pulling the trigger of his silenced gun twice, and he watched the shadow collapse to the ground. Tarzan hoped the fall did not hurt Sophia, but his instincts were right. It wasn't a civilian he just killed; it was another of Don Castillo's men.

Tarzan walked warily to the body and followed the same routine as with the first hitman. He checked his ID, and this time, he hit pay dirt. He found five hundred thousand lira, which was about eight hundred dollars in American money and a few business cards in the wallet, and it pleased him to see that one business card was Don Castillo's. Tarzan put the wallet back in the man's pants pocket, kept the money, took his weapon, and stuck it in his belt. Then he brushed the dirt from Sophia's coat with his hands, and he apologized to her for shoving her to the ground. "I'm sorry for shoving you, Sophia, but I was afraid that gunman would kill you, because you were directly in his line of fire." He took her arm. "I apologize for having been rough with you before when you grabbed hold of my arm, but

The Sicilian Caper

if I had to use my gun, I needed my arm free, and you were hanging on to it."

She nodded in understanding. "It was foolish of me. I should have known better. I thought we were both about to be killed by the second gunman, and I was scared out of my wits. You surprised me when you shot him. I'm still shaking from that horrible experience, but I am also glad you killed him. I don't know how you knew he was there, because I never heard a thing. You saved both of our lives, and you rid the world of those two beasts."

Tarzan took Sophia's arm, and they walked to her home, keeping close to the trees and staying in the shadows, doing their best not to make a suitable target in case a third shooter was stalking them. So far, Don Castillo and his men did not know where Red and his men were hiding, and they wanted to keep it that way. Don Castillo must have assigned men to watch several places where Red or his men might show up. They got lucky tonight; well, maybe not so lucky because Tarzan and Sophia were the ones who walked back to her home, while the other two men were back in the weeds dancing with the devil, in the shrubbery in the alley's rear where Tarzan dumped them.

Tarzan and Sophia paused in front of her home for a moment while Tarzan scanned the area for a shadow. Nothing moved, nothing was out of place. He motioned with his head to the door, and Sophia opened it, and they walked in. Tarzan told Sophia to shut the lights. She did, and he pulled the shade aside and took one last long look outside, scanning the street near the house for threats. Seeing none, he put the shade back in place and he motioned for Sophia to put the lights back on. Red witnessed Tarzan's cautious routine, and he knew something was amiss. "Out with it, Tarzan. What happened out there?"

But it was Sophia who answered Red. "Oh, Red. Tarzan was wonderful. He saved our lives. Two of Don Castillo's men were waiting near the blacksmith's shop, waiting to kill us, but Tarzan killed both of them instead. I was never so frightened in my life."

"Tell me about it, Tarzan, and start at the beginning and leave nothing out."

Tarzan placed both of the dead men's guns on the coffee

table, and he handed Red back his Colt. He did the same with the money he took from the dead gunmen. "You might find this useful, Red." Tarzan handed Red Don Castillo's business card. Red studied the information the card had on it and smiled. "This is good, Tarzan. The card has Castillo's phone number and address on it. I think I'll call him tomorrow. Or maybe we'll drop in on him and surprise the bastard, but don't worry, I'll think of something interesting to do with him."

Tarzan knew the Don's business card was important to Red, so he just nodded, and then he gave Red a step-by-step account of what happened after he made the transatlantic phone call to Fred Thompson. "The plane is yours, Red, but he wants you to send him a check for thirty thousand dollars as a good faith deposit. Plus, you'll agree to house your plane in one of Thompson's hangers, and have his company do all the plane's maintenance. A new Lockheed Jetstar costs two million eight hundred thousand dollars. Fred told me he'd sell you the jet for two million one hundred thousand dollars, minus the money you owe him for the extra days you're using the jet, so you'll get the jet for two million dollars."

"Call Captain Frankie and get his opinion on the price. If he tells you it's a fair price, I'll buy it, but don't use Sophia's phone. They may have tapped it," Red said.

"Christ Red. That means I'll have to use the payphone by the blacksmith's shop."

"That's right. Use the payphone by the blacksmith's shop. Don't worry; you won't go alone. Pissclam will go with you to watch your back."

"Wait a minute, Red," Sophia interrupted. "There are still two dead bodies near that payphone. I'll drive Tarzan and Sammy to a payphone down the road a bit. It's safer using that payphone." Sophia used Pissclam's given name. She called him Sammy instead of Pissclam, his nickname, because she was a lady, and ladies didn't use that sort of language in front of men.

Joey Boy sauntered into the room looking much better than he had in the past three days. Sophia noticed him leaning against her bedroom door. She walked up to him and, without saying a word to him, she felt his forehead for fever, and it felt normal. "Come with me. I want to take your temperature. Your color is

The Sicilian Caper

back, and you no longer have that white pasty look, but I want to be sure. She placed her thermometer in his mouth and waited. Then she removed the thermometer and read it. "Normal," she said, satisfied. Then she examined his wounds. There was no infection, and that pleased her. She cleaned his wounds and changed his dressings. "How do you feel, Joey Boy?"

"I feel wonderful, doctor, especially having you fuss over me."

Sophia blushed, and she looked at Joey Boy again. But this time not as a patient, but as a very handsome man, and something stirred in her. She hadn't been close to a man since they killed her fiancé, and that was four years ago. Joey Boy could read a female as good as any man, and he sensed Sophia's interest in him, and he felt good about it because he genuinely liked her. She was a fine woman, different from most of the girls he knew. He'd like to get to know her better, but that would depend on how things went with Don Castillo. He was still too weak to assist his friends if they went to war with the Don, but he felt himself getting stronger each day.

CHAPTER 14

Red listened to every word Tarzan told him, and when he finished, Red knew he was the owner of the jet he leased. He also knew that Don Castillo was a dead man. Red went over various scenarios in his mind. He thought of sending the jet back and then have it return to Sicily with eight or ten of his men, as backup when he attempted to eliminate Don Castillo, but he quickly dismissed that idea. If he was back in Queens, he could call on a small army to take care of Don Castillo, but here, he'd have to handle the Don with the resources he had on hand, and when he accomplished that, then he'd deal with Enzo Batto.

"What are you planning to do now, boss?" Pissclam asked.

"We're going to pay a visit to that murdering piece of shit Don Castillo."

"How are you going to find where his headquarters are, boss?" Pissclam asked.

"Tarzan gave me his business card he took from the man he killed. But before we do that, we're going to pay Enzo's cousin Mario a visit at his tobacco shop, and with a little persuasion, he'll tell us things that are not on the Don's card. He'll tell us where we can find his rat cousin. It's time we began acting like wolves instead of sheep."

"Are you planning to go without me?" Joey Boy said, leaning against the doorjamb, barely able to stand from the doorway to Sophia's bedroom.

Sophia jumped up and ran to him to prevent him from falling. "What's wrong with you? Are you crazy? You shouldn't be out of bed, now get back in that bed. Do you think I tended to your wounds only to see you drop dead on me after all of my efforts to save you? Do you?"

The Sicilian Caper

The men laughed at the way Sophia chastised her patient, and they laughed harder at Joey Boy's discomfort at being put in his place by this pretty young lady. "And you were so nice a few minutes ago when you took my temperature," he told Sophia with a hangdog look on his face, causing more laughter from his friends.

She laughed. "Don't feel bad because you can't go with your friends. Think of it this way. I need someone here to protect me in case Don Castillo sends someone here to see if I'm sheltering Red or his men."

Joey Boy smiled. "Well, Sophia, in that case, I'll be happy to stay here to protect you from those evil men." She laughed at the incongruity of his statement, but she loved hearing him say it nonetheless.

Sophia led Joey Boy back into the bedroom. She told him she wanted to clean his wounds, and she wanted to replace his dressings with clean bandages. Red watched them disappear into the bedroom and close the door behind them, when there was a tapping at the front door. The men pulled their guns and took defensive positions. Red opened the door an inch, and it relieved him to see an older woman standing there. Red opened the door all the way and invited the old lady in. She surveyed the room and couldn't help noticing the men watching TV.

When the men saw it was an old lady who knocked, they relaxed, put their guns away, and sat back down. "No, signore. I came here to shop for Sophia. I wanted to ask her what she wanted me to buy for her."

Red put his hand in his pocket and pulled out a roll of bills. He peeled off a number of lira and handed it to the woman. "Me and the boys are looking forward to a good home-cooked Italian meal, so buy a lot of pasta and make sauce for us, and buy a steak for Joey Boy. The beef will give him strength. I want to surprise Sophia by having her enjoy a wonderful feast without knowing it's for her. If you are interested, I will pay you to cook the meal for us."

The old lady smiled appreciatively. "There is no need to pay me for something I would gladly do for nothing. I will buy the food and I will cook it for you. It will be my pleasure."

"Then you must join us for dinner. Bring your family too."

"It's just me, signore. My children are grown and have their own families, and my husband passed away last year, so I am alone."

"But you will join us for dinner tonight, I insist."

"Thank you for inviting me, and yes, I would love to join you for dinner. Now you must excuse me. I have a lot of shopping to do and then I still have to cook the meal. I'll be careful though. I'll buy some of what I need now, and later I will go back and buy the rest of the food from his wife, so no one will know how much food I bought. I better be going now, because I don't want to disappoint you."

"Buy everything you need. Don't scrimp and get anything else you feel is necessary for the best meal this side of heaven, and buy a few bottles of the best wine you can get."

The old lady laughed. "It may cost more than the lira you gave me."

Red peeled more lira from his bankroll and handed it to the old lady. "Don't worry about the money. Just buy the best food and wine available."

The old lady took the lira and smiled coyly at Red. "Sophia will surely be surprised tonight. I can't wait to see her face when she sees all the food."

"When you have the food ready to be served, tap on the door just like you did now, and we'll usher Sophia into the bedroom door while I let you in. We'll set the table, so all you have to do is bring the food in, and when that's done, we'll bring Sophia back in. She'll know something is up, but she won't know what, so we'll just say we have a surprise for her."

When the old lady left, Tarzan motioned to Red to follow him outside to the back patio. When they were outside, they sat down at a small patio table. Red knew Tarzan wanted to discuss the situation they were in, so while he waited for Tarzan to broach the subject, he pulled out his cigar wallet and removed two cigars. He lit his, then he handed one to Tarzan and gave Tarzan his gold Zippo lighter for Tarzan to light his cigar. "What's on your mind, Tarzan?"

"We need to come up with a plan to take down Don Castillo, and we have to do it with the men we have. There must be payback for them killing Tic-Tok." Tarzan's eyes bored into

The Sicilian Caper

Red's. "The Don has to pay for killing my friend," Tarzan said coldly.

"I hear you, Tarzan, and I feel the same way."

"The problem is Don Castillo must have an army of men who are on his payroll. How do we overcome that?" Tarzan asked.

"We chop off the head of the snake, and the body will die," Red said.

"It's too bad we have to go through all this bullshit just to get to Enzo."

"You got that right, Tarzan. Enzo has a powerful friend in Don Castillo, but I'm going to bypass the Don and instead find Enzo, kill him, and then we'll head home."

"That's fine, Red, but how are we going to find Enzo without going through the Don?"

"Enzo's cousin Mario will tell us. The guy's legit. He runs a tiny store in a little village. Mario is a simple man and he won't be used to men like us. He'll talk. His choices are limited... talk or die."

"That sounds good to me, Red, but don't you think that Don Castillo might have left one or two men with Enzo, and he may have left a man with his cousin figuring it was likely that one of us might go to the tobacco shop to ask Mario questions about his cousin Enzo?"

"When we get to his shop, we have to be extra vigilant. I suspect that one or more of the Don's men are watching the tobacco shop just like they did when we tried to break into the store, so we must be careful when we go there."

"When do you figure on doing this, Red?"

"We'll do it tomorrow. Tonight, we'll enjoy the surprise dinner for Sophia, her friend and neighbor Rosa, the old lady next door is cooking the meal for us."

A tap on the door told Red that the old lady was here with the meal, but just in case it was an uninvited guest, Red pulled out his gun and waved Pissclam toward the door. Pissclam took a position at the side of the door in case it was one of the Don's men and not the old lady. Red pulled the curtain aside and relaxed. It was the next-door neighbor with a cartload of food. Before he let the old lady in, he told Tarzan, "We have to do this fast. Stand by the door, Tarzan, and make sure Sophia remains in the room with Joey Boy." Red let the old lady in and ordered Pissclam to help her bring the food in quickly. They'd already set the table. Now all they needed was the food placed on the table and the rest on the rolling stand Sophia's neighbor used to roll the food with. They dimmed the lights and lit the two candles on either end of the table. The table looked like a picture, even though it was a race to get the table set quickly.

Red looked at the old lady and apologized for not knowing her name. "My name is Rosa Delgado, but just Rosa will be fine."

"Hi Rosa, my name is Red, and these are my friends. That big man is Trenchie and the good-looking guy over there is Tarzan, and Sophia is taking care of Joey Boy. Now later, I'll give you a test on the names I just told you."

Rosa's eyes widened. "A test? I cannot take a test."

Red laughed. "Relax, Rosa, I was just kidding with you."

Rosa visibly relaxed. "Good. I no do good with tests."

"Tarzan, dim the lights and call Sophia in here. Tell her something happened, that'll get her in here quick."

Tarzan opened the door a few inches and called out to Sophia. "Sophia, something happened. You better come in here quick."

Sophia burst into the room, expecting to see a catastrophe. Instead, she saw a dimly lit room; the table set with the most wonderful variety of foods, her neighbor Rosa, and Tarzan, Trenchie, Pissclam, Sal, and even Joey Boy sitting expectantly at the table. "What's this?" Sophia said with tears of happiness rolling down her cheeks.

"Sit down at the head of the table, Sophia. You can thank Rosa for shopping for the food, and then cooking the meal to perfection." Rosa blushed at the compliment. "Me and the boys wanted to do something nice for you, to show our appreciation for having saved Joey Boy's life, and for the loving professional care you're still giving him." The men stood, and clapped, and then they lined up, and one at a time, they kissed her on her cheek. "Please sit down Sophia, and enjoy your food, and share this special night with us."

Sophia looked at Red and then she looked into the faces of

The Sicilian Caper

each man, and their eyes locked on one another's. "Thank you for this wonderful night. It will be a memory I shall never forget. I never expected this, but now that it is happening, all I can say is thank you to all of you seated at my table."

Rosa reached for a napkin before the tears fell like a spring shower. Sophia became as emotional as Rosa, and she followed her example and picked up her napkin, and then she, too, dabbed at her eyes as she looked up at the men at her table. "I don't know how to thank you for this night. Until this moment, this is the most unforgettable night of my life."

"Well said, Sophia," Joey Boy said.

The men stood and raised their glasses. "To Sophia." And then they sat down.

"Now let's eat." Joey Boy said, reaching for a steak.

"Look at him reaching for the steak. There's nothing wrong with him," Trenchie said.

The man laughed and Sophia felt a genuine affection for each of the men.

After dinner, when they were clearing the table, Red motioned to Pissclam and mouthed for him to bring him the small leather pouch he took with him from Queens and carried with him from the plane. The pouch contained a few select pieces of jewelry they found in the safe of the Golden Spike Casino after Red bought it. Red reached in the pouch and took out an object wrapped in an expensive silk napkin with two black-gold delicate straps holding the handkerchief closed. It contained a woman's gold Rolex and Red placed the beautiful silk handkerchief in his pocket, then he handed the leather pouch back to Pissclam.

As the night wound down and Rosa stood to leave, Red thanked her and he asked her if she had enough money for the food she bought earlier. Rosa misunderstood what he meant, and she apologized for not giving him his change. Red put his hand over hers, and he shook his head. "That's not what I'm asking you, Rosa," and he placed two one-hundred-dollar bills in her hand, and then he closed her hand. "That's for what you did today. It is as if you read my mind. You shopped for the food, cooked the food, set the food on the table, served the food, helped clean up. Sophia is lucky to have a friend like you. The money is what I would have paid to have someone do what you did for us today. I want you to have it, so don't argue with me. I'm bigger than you."

She laughed at his little joke and then impulsively she hugged him and kissed him on the cheek. "Thank you, Mr. Red. I appreciate the thought, and I can use the money."

Unknown to Red, Sophia watched the entire scene unfold. When Red turned to join his men, he saw her, and he knew she witnessed the interaction that just took place between Rosa and him. "That was very nice of you, Red. Rosa's a good person and you made her feel important and what you told her made her happy."

"Were you happy tonight?" he asked her.

"Yes, very. I wasn't lying when I said this was the happiest day of my life."

Red smiled. "Well, your happiest day isn't over yet. The day still holds a surprise for you."

"What do you mean, Red?"

"Me and the boys have a little something we want to give to you."

"I want nothing more, Red. You've done enough for me, and you made me happy."

"Well, me and the boys like to make you happy. He reached into his pocket and handed her a small bundle of tissue paper with something wrapped inside of it. "I'm sorry we don't have a box for our gift, so the gift wrapped in tissue paper will have to do."

She opened the tissue paper and gasped when she saw what they wrapped in the paper. "My God Red. I can't take the watch. It must be worth a fortune."

"All the more reason for you to have it. It's something to remember who gave it to you, and to remember us when we're gone."

She studied the beautiful, expensive gold watch from every angle before putting it on her wrist. "I had nothing as lovely or expensive as this watch. It's so beautiful, I can't take my eyes off of it."

To Red, it was easy come, easy go. He got the watch for nothing, and he enjoyed seeing the reaction to the Rolex Sophia

The Sicilian Caper

had, the beautiful young lady who had saved Joey Boy's life, and had given shelter to Red and his men, expecting nothing in return. This girl was special, and he wanted to do more for her. He thought about how she had to drop out of medical school, because she didn't have enough money to complete her education. So he silently vowed he'd send her the money to finish her medical education. He justified the intended gift by telling himself that she saved Joey Boy's life and she took him and his men in, even when she didn't know the men they were. Red laughed inwardly. If he got lucky, either Enzo or Don Castillo would not only pay for her education, they'd pay for his jet too, because if he found a stash of cash, it might be enough to pay for her education plus a sizable down payment on the plane. If they found no cash, then he was no worse off than he was now. Red was a criminal who controlled many, if not all, the Queens rackets. He was a hard-hearted taker, and not a giver, but like the American Indian, he respected courage, and he returned a favor when one was given. Ten years ago, he would never have thought of giving any of his money to anyone, but when Yip died, he left Red millions in property and cash, and Red took his place as the boss of the Queens mob. Red now owned movie studios, Las Vegas casinos, car dealerships, and other profitable businesses. Money was no longer a concern for Red, so by paying for Sophia's medical education, not only would he not miss the money, he could use the gift as a tax write-off, and besides... he knew Joey Boy was sweet on her, so it would be better to make a good impression on her. Now that he decided, he felt a lot better. He'd ask her for and receive a total on her tuition, and as soon as he returned to the States, he'd instruct his accountant to send a check directly to the university for the total amount Sophia owed. With that settled, Red felt a lot lighter. Now he could concentrate on finding Enzo without encountering any pain in the ass outside pressure.

Red's alarm went off at seven in the morning. When he walked into the kitchen, it surprised him to see Sophia cooking a stack of pancakes. "Good morning, Red. There's fresh coffee on the stove, so pour yourself a cup and I'll bring you a stack of pancakes with real maple syrup." The men woke up to the smell of pancakes and fresh coffee percolating and the smell of pancakes wafting throughout the house.

"I don't know how you do it, Sophia. I mean, feeding all the men and always having enough food in the house."

"I have enough food to feed you men, because you gave me enough money to buy the food. Now stop worrying, and take a seat at the table and I'll bring you a plate of the tastiest homemade pancakes you will ever eat."

Red pulled out his roll of bills and peeled off another two hundred dollars. He left the money on the sink beside the stove. He was afraid if he gave it to Sophia, she'd refuse it, telling him to put the money back in his pocket, that he had given her enough money.

After breakfast, Red told his men to arm themselves. "We're leaving for the tobacco shop as soon as we finish going over our plans."

"Do you want me to call Captain Frankie, Red?"

Pissclam asked. "Hell no. If anything happens to him, who's going to fly us home? Let him stay where he is, but call him and tell him to stay close to a phone. We may have to leave Sicily at a run."

"Okay, boss. I'll call him now."

"Sal, where did you park the car?" Red asked.

"I parked it in the alley behind the house."

"Get it. We're going to drive to the tobacco shop in a few minutes, and we'll park the car in the alley behind the building. I saw it the first time we went there, and the alley is large enough to park our car in without being seen. The problem is getting there without being seen by the lookout in the store."

"We can drive around the block and approach the store from behind. I think we can sneak in the driveway behind the store without being seen, and we're armed, so if they spot us and open fire, we can fire back. We have more men and more firepower than they have, so why should we be worried?"

"What you say makes sense, Sal, but do you really think we can we get to the driveway behind the store without being seen?"

"We can try, Red. And besides, who gives a shit if they see us? They want a fight, then let's give them one."

Red laughed. "Good point, Sal, and you're right. If they

The Sicilian Caper

want a fight, let's give them a fight they'll never forget."

With Pissclam driving, the car moved slowly into the alley behind the tobacco store, with no one apparently aware of the car being there. "So far, so good," Tarzan said.

"Park under the tree alongside that van," Red ordered, pointing to a large tree with hanging branches. The men had their weapons out in case they had to use them.

"If they left a man in the store, then he surely had to see us, but we can't be sure," Tarzan said.

"Well, there's only one way to find out if there's a lookout, and that's entering the store and see who's there. If it's just Mario, then we have it made, but if there's a lookout, we'll have to kill him before he kills us," Red added.

"I'll go in there and find out who's in there. Here's my gun, Red. Give me your silenced gun. If I have to plug someone, I don't want to alert the neighborhood." Tarzan stepped into the store and looked cautiously around. No one was there but a little man standing on a stool placing cigar boxes on shelves.

"Just a moment and I'll be right with you." Mario finished stacking the cigar boxes and stepped off the stool and turned to help Tarzan, and that was when he noticed he wasn't a regular customer, as evidenced by the gun in his hand. He was a stranger looking for Enzo. "Madre mia. You cannot be here. You must leave before Muro returns."

Tarzan walked to the door and Mario mistakenly thought he heeded his warning and was leaving. Instead, Tarzan waved to Red and the men and motioned for them to hurry into the store. "They have a man watching for strangers, but he's not here now. The owner expects him to return at any moment and he's nervous as hell about it," Tarzan informed Red.

"Let's have a talk with Mario while we have the opportunity."

The rough-looking men approached the frightened little storekeeper and semi-surrounded him. "Pissclam, keep an eye out for the man they stationed here. He'll be returning here at any minute. Let me know the moment you see him."

"Okay, boss." Pissclam took a position near the front window, watching the few passersby for a threat.

Red's look bored right through Mario, and the little man

was frightened of these hard men. He didn't want trouble from Enzo or Don Castillo, and certainly not with these men, but what could he do? He finally found the nerve to ask the stranger with the red hair, in a trembling voice, "How can I help you? What do you want from me?"

Red gave him an amiable smile. "All we want from you is for you to tell me where I can find your cousin Enzo. Tell us that and we'll leave here." Red put his arm around his shoulder as if they were old friends. "Look, Mario." Red noticed the surprised look on Mario's face that he knew his name. "Yes. I know your name. In fact, I know a lot about you, Mario. I'm usually a peaceful man, but when someone wrongs me, then I'm not so peaceful. Now look at me. You must tell me where Enzo is hiding. Tell me that and we'll go, and you won't see us again."

Mario's pained expression told Red that he wanted to tell them what they wanted to know, but he was more frightened of Enzo and Don Castillo than him. So Red used a different approach. Red had a code he lived by, which was, you never hurt a civilian, or someone's family if they could avoid it. But Mario had no way of knowing this, so Red used it to frighten the little man, and Mario would never know he was bluffing. "Look, Mario. I know you don't want to tell us where your cousin is, but if you don't tell me, then you'll force me to hurt your family, which I really don't enjoy doing, so spare yourself and your lovely family the pain you will force me to bring to them. Tell me where Enzo is, and if he discovers it was you who told us, you'll have the perfect excuse. You told us what we wanted to know in order to protect your family." Red locked his eyes on Mario's. Red gave a slight nod to Rocco, who was a native Sicilian, and he displayed a long stiletto. "Does it have to come to this, Mario? Are you really going to force me to use this on you, and then use it on your family?" Red tilted his head toward Mario, and Rocco raised the stiletto as he approached Mario. "Last chance, Mario." Red was willing to have Rocco cut the little man just enough to scare him, but he didn't want him seriously hurt. After all, he was just an innocent bystander, with important information Red needed. Rocco raised the knife as if he were about to pluck Mario's right eye from his face,

The Sicilian Caper

when Mario raised his hands.

"No... Please don't hurt me. I'll tell you what you want to know."

"That's better, Mario. I'm glad you didn't make me hurt you. It would have ruined my day. Now tell me where Enzo is hiding." Mario told Red about Enzo's cave and how it was almost impossible to find without someone there to show them.

Suddenly, Pissclam called out to Red, "A guy is heading toward the store, Red. He'll be here in a minute."

"Everybody hide in the back. Let the guy come in and then we'll grab him."

The man walked into the empty tobacco store and approached Mario. "Sorry it took me so long. I had to change the battery in my car. Did you notice any strangers, Mario?"

"Yes, he did," Tarzan said, walking from behind the curtain separating the front retail part of the business from the storeroom, and to a small office brandishing his gun.

The man raised his arms. "Do you speak English?" Red asked.

The man had a confused look on his face, but Tarzan repeated what Red asked the man. The man shook his head. "He doesn't speak English, Red. What do you want me to ask him?"

"Ask him his name."

"Muro."

"Tell Muro I want him to take us to Enzo's hideout."

The man shook his head vigorously when Tarzan told him what Red asked of him. "He won't do it, Red. He said he's not a snitch and he won't betray his friends."

"Ask Muro if Enzo is a friend of his."

"He said Enzo isn't his friend, but Tomasso, the man protecting Enzo, is his friend."

"Tell him we won't hurt his friend. Let him know the reason I came all the way from America to Sicily to kill Enzo was because he murdered my father, and I'm following the law of the Sicilian vendetta. Ask him if he would act differently if Enzo had killed his father."

Muro didn't know Enzo, but if Enzo killed his father, he sure as hell would have issued a vendetta against him. They expected you to retaliate if someone killed a member of your

111

family. In Sicily, they expected the oldest male to take charge and seek revenge, which most likely was the father, but if they killed the father, then the vendetta called for the oldest son to kill the man who killed his father. If the oldest son was to die in the attempt to fulfill the vendetta, then the vendetta fell to the next oldest son, and so on, until there were no sons left to carry out the vendetta. Muro listened as Tarzan told him the reason Red came to Sicily, and when Tarzan finished explaining the reason Red was here, it tore Muro. He had a duty to fulfill, but he hated the thought that a man could kill someone's father and not pay the price. The man asked Red a question in Sicilian, and Red knew enough Sicilian to make out what the man asked him, but Tarzan, who spoke Sicilian, interpreted the question for Red. "He wants to know if there are any other sons in your family who could fulfill the vendetta?"

"Tell him I'm the only son that can honor the vendetta."

The man asked Tarzan another question, and he turned to face Red. "He wants your word that if he tells you what you want to know, you'll keep your word and let him go."

Red sighed. "All right. Tell him I'm a man of honor, and if he shows me where I can find Enzo, then I'll have no reason to kill him. All I want is Enzo. If he tells me that, then he has my word, he'll be free to go." The Sicilian shook his head and shrugged, and then he said something to Tarzan. Red knew that something just happened, and he didn't like hearing what Tarzan was about to tell him. "Red, Muro said he has no problem taking you to Enzo, but he fears what Don Castillo will do to him when he finds out he betrayed him."

Red actually liked the Sicilian being afraid, and he'd use that fear convincing Muro to show him a way into the castle.

"Ask him if Don Castillo was no longer a problem, would that make him feel better?"

The man nodded vigorously as he said a few words to Tarzan. "If the Don was no longer a threat, then yes, he'd feel much better."

"Ask him if he knows a way we can get into the castle with no one knowing about it?"

They exchanged words between Tarzan, and the Sicilian, and then Tarzan smiled. "He told me there's an old entrance in

The Sicilian Caper

a cave that was used mainly as an escape route in case the castle was under attack. When the castle was no longer under a threat of being attacked, two hundred years ago, they sealed that old entrance by placing a thick metal gate over the entrance, to make sure no one entered the cave. Muro said with a few good men and some effort, they can reopen it."

"Good, that's what I wanted to hear, and that's what we'll do. We'll reopen the metal gate, get into the castle, and we'll surprise the Don without him ever knowing we breached his castle."

Red turned to Mario and pulled him aside where Tarzan and the Sicilian couldn't hear what they were saying.

"If this man can get me into the castle, then you're off the hook. There are still a few questions I have for you. Aside from finding Enzo, I want to know if besides the entrance to the castle Muro told us about, do you know a different way into Don Castillo's castle? There must be a better way of getting inside his castle than through the metal gate covering the cave. You have lived here all of your life and you must have heard stories from some of the old timers who knew how to get that castle."

"You have heard Muro say you can get in by using the old cave entrance. He will take you to the entrance and he will show you the way in, but no one knows where they hid the scroll that shows you where the traps are located."

"I don't like hearing about traps. That's why you must show us another way into the castle that won't alert Castillo of our presence."

"I can't tell you what I don't know, but there may be another way. There is an old man who used to be the head of security for Don Castillo, but that was many, many years ago. But he was the man in charge of security, so maybe he knows where they hid that scroll."

"Come on, let's go talk to this man."

Mario shook his head. "The man is an old man, and he's in a nursing home. He may not even be alive, although I haven't been told of his passing, and I get all the gossip in my store."

"How old is this guy?" Red asked.

"He's one hundred and one years old, but his mind was sharp the last time I spoke to him. He likes the old thin Italian cigars, the real strong ones, that you Americans know as the Guinea Stinker. Very few Americans can smoke that cigar without becoming nauseous."

"He sounds like my kind of man. Let's take a ride and see if he's still in the nursing home."

"I have no one to watch my store while I'm gone."

"I'll leave Tarzan here. He'll handle your customers, as long as you marked the price of every item on it."

"Yes, I always write the price on the items I sell."

"Good, because Tarzan speaks the Sicilian dialect fluently, so there shouldn't be a problem. Besides, we won't waste time. We'll be back right after we talk to the old man."

It was a fifteen-minute ride to the old sanitarium that was now used as a retirement home for the elderly. The old man was alive and the nurse at the desk gave them his room number.

The old man was in a wheelchair, asleep on the rear porch facing the gardens.

"Dominick, wake up. Dominick."

The old man's eyes fluttered open. "Who is here? Who calls me?"

"It's Mario from the tobacco shop, Dominick, and I brought you something."

"You brought me something. What is it? What did you bring me?" The old man was suddenly alive, acting like a kid again. Mario reached into his pocket and took out the strong Italian cigars Dominick loved. His eyes widened when he saw them. "Oh, Mario, you don't know how I longed for a good cigar, and you brought some to me. Push me out onto the terrace. I want to smoke a cigar. There's nothing I enjoy more than a good cigar." Since Tarzan wasn't there to translate what the old man said, Red managed to make himself understood and could pick up what the old man said with his limited use of the old language. He wheeled the old man onto the terrace, and he pulled out a cigar of his own, lit it, and then put his lit lighter under Dominick's cigar for him to light. "Ahhh," Dominick sighed contentedly. "Now that I have my cigar, I feel like the Dons of old where, if they were happy, they would grant favors to their guests. I will grant you a favor. What is it you want from me, Mario? Tell me, and if it is in my power, I will give it to

The Sicilian Caper

you."

"What I'm about to tell you must remain between us... agreed?"

"This sounds serious, so I am intrigued by what you are about to ask me. So tell me, what do you want from me?"

"Information, Dominick. Since you were in charge of security for Don Castillo, you must know things no one else does."

"So? You still haven't told me what you want from me."

Red thought to himself, *this old man is still sharp as a tack*, but Mario's voice interrupted his thoughts. "We are going to enter the Don's castle using the old cave that has been sealed for a hundred years."

"Two hundred years," Dominick added. "How will you get in?"

"We'll have to cut the old lock and open the iron grating covering the cave."

The old man waved his hand. "No need to do that. You might need a can of penetrating oil to loosen the metal joints, but you won't need to cut the lock. There are trees directly in front of the opening. Go to the closest tree, step behind it, and count off ten paces and then dig. About a foot down, you will find a metal box. A key to the lock is in the box, plus a sealed scroll. The seal is Don Castillo's great-great-grandfather's seal. In the old days, the castle was a refuge from warring principalities, so they built their castle at the peak of the mountain. While they were constructing the castle, they discovered a series of caves. One cave led up to where the castle was being built. When they discovered the sloping cave system, they incorporated the cave into their castle design. They knew from the beginning that it would make an excellent escape route in case of attack by another prince. But the builders went a step further. They knew the prince and his family would get safely away in case of an attack by following the underground cave to the exit in the forest. The problem was there was always the possibility that their enemies could learn of the cave entrance, and use it to gain entrance to the castle and kill the prince and his family. Prince Castillo's great-great-grandfather used the cave entrance sparingly, but he used it until about two hundred years ago. The old principalities and princes died off and Sicilian aristocrats took their places. Gaining entrance should prove to be no problem to you, but the safeguards placed for the princes and his families protection could prove to be a problem to you if you don't have the scroll to point out what to look for, and where they hid the traps."

"How many traps are there, Dominick?"

"Three or four traps, so you must be careful and do not take chances. Do not enter the cave if you don't have the scroll. Now I've told you what you need to know. Let me enjoy my cigar."

"Thank you for your help, Dominick. Next time, I'll bring you the box of cigars."

Dominick chuckled. "Then you had better come back sooner rather than later... if you know what I mean."

When the men left the nursing home, Red tapped Mario. "Let's get a shovel and drive to the cave. No one should be there now, so we shouldn't have anyone interfering or stopping us from digging a hole."

"I have a shovel in my truck. Let's stop by the store and I'll get it. Make a left and pull onto that road," Mario said, pointing to a narrow dirt road that could hardly be seen from the main road. The road was nothing more than a game trail, just wide enough for one car. If a car came in the opposite direction, it would force one car to back up, until they came to a clearing that they could pull into, to allow the other car to pass before they could continue their journey. The road widened about a half mile from the entrance. "Pull into that clearing, Red. The cave is there, but it's hidden by the thick foliage." Red pulled the truck into the clearing and shut the ignition. "Follow me," Mario said. They continued along a different path for about thirty feet, when suddenly, a mountain loomed ominously in front of them. "The cave is just around that bend, and like Enzo's cave, it's hidden by thick shrubs, but it's there." The two men walked the short distance until Mario put his hand out for Red to stop. "We're here. The cave opening is right there," he said, pointing at the shrubs. He turned and quickly located the first tree from the cave's entrance. "Although you can't see the entrance to the cave, it's right in front of us, and this is the closest tree to the entrance. Come. Now we count ten paces and

The Sicilian Caper

dig for the metal box."

They counted ten paces off and, after digging about a foot, the shovel struck metal. "It looks as if Dominick was right. He led us right to the box with the key to the entrance to the cave. Let's clear the box and see if the key is in it, like Dominick said." They cleared the dirt around the metal box and pulled it out. It had a simple lock on it, which was easily snapped open by one downward swipe of the shovel. Mario was wholeheartedly into this adventure.

The box, when opened, revealed two items. One was a large key wrapped in a cloth to protect it from the elements and the many years underground. The second item was an old scroll sealed with red wax. Red broke the seal and opened the scroll. It had a map of the cave's route from the opening at ground level to the hidden entrance into the castle. It relieved Red to see four large red X's at intervals along the caves snaking route from the opening below to the top exit. He would study the map when he got back to Sophia's house. Now that he had his way into the castle, there was no hurry. He could take care of Enzo and get that out of the way. It was one more obstacle that he'd be happy to be rid of. With Enzo out of the way, he could concentrate on entering the castle and eliminating the Don. He would have ignored the Don, but that changed when his men killed Tic-Tok and shot Joey Boy all to hell. Now it was a matter of honor to have revenge on the man who killed Tic-Tok and his father. An unsanctioned vendetta, so to speak, but a vendetta that had to be answered for, none the less.

What do you want to do, Red?" Mario asked.

"Let's go back to the store. I want to take some of my men with me when we go into the cave." Then he had a thought. "Mario, does Don Castillo know about the cave?"

Mario shrugged. "Who knows? But he obviously knows the history of his castle, so he must know about the cave's emergency escape route."

"Was the cave sealed during his lifetime?"

Mario thought for a few seconds. "I believe they sealed the cave during his great-grandfather's time, or maybe earlier."

"Tomorrow, I'd like to stop by the old folks' home and bring Dominick the box of cigars I promised him. I want to ask him a few questions about Castillo and his castle, and while I'm there, I'll show him the scroll and ask him about the four traps and ask him what I should be wary of."

"Good idea, Red. If you don't mind, I would like to go with you. He knows me and he trusts me. I promise I won't get in your way."

Red laughed. "I've been trying to get you to talk and to trust me, and now I can't get rid of you, but sure, you can come with me, and don't let this give you a big head, but I would also enjoy your company."

Mario puffed up his chest upon hearing Red's compliment. "Thank you, Red. I enjoy your company as well."

"That settles it. I'll pick you up tomorrow morning, and we'll visit Dominick at the old folks' home." Then Red thought of Enzo, and he didn't like leaving loose ends unattended to, and Enzo was a loose end that had to be dealt with before he could think of doing anything else. Red realized that he couldn't have his father's killer remain alive, so he could devise a time and place to kill him too. Using the cave to enter Castillo's castle would have to wait. Enzo was the priority. He had to be dealt with first, and the sooner the better. He'd talk to Muro and use his knowledge to kill Enzo. "Let's go back to your shop, Mario. I want to ask Muro a few questions."

CHAPTER 15

The next morning when Red walked into Mario's tobacco shop, it relieved him to see Muro there talking to Tarzan. They both stopped talking when Red approached them. "Today's the day, Muro. Today, you will take me to Enzo's hideout." Tarzan translated what Red said. Muro looked nervous. "What's wrong? You look nervous."

"I am, Red. After I take you to Enzo's hideout, everyone in Sicily will know it was me that betrayed Enzo, and then my life won't be worth a bag of salt."

Red didn't like where this conversation was going. "You will do it, Muro. You know that."

"Yes, I know that, and I will do it, but I have a question for you."

Red narrowed his eyes. "Go ahead, ask your question."

"When Enzo is dead, I can't remain in Sicily. I'd like to go back to America with you, and if you'll have me, I'd like to join your organization."

"What about your family? Won't they miss you?"

"I have no family, Red, just an uncle. That's why I'd like to start over and work with you in New York."

Red thought about Muro's request, and he saw no reason he couldn't come with them. There was room in the jet, and he could always use another good man he could trust, and Muro wasn't afraid to use his gun, which in Red's business was a required necessity. "All right, Muro. After I deal with Enzo, go home, pack your suitcase and meet us at Mario's place, and we'll take you to America with us. Now you're going to show us where Enzo's hideout is."

"Remember, Red, you promised not to hurt Tomasso."

"I'll keep my promise as long as he doesn't shoot at me and the boys."

"That's no problem. He'll call me at Mario's in a little while, and I'll tell him I'm coming up there and you'll be with me."

"I don't like that, Muro. He's there to protect Enzo. He'll shoot us as soon as we get close enough. I don't enjoy taking chances and your friend represents danger to me. Think of something else, because if we go there tomorrow, your friend is likely to get himself killed. Tell him to call in sick tomorrow."

Muro didn't respond right away, but then he seemed to decide. "Red, I have another question for you. Could you use two good men instead of just one good man?" Red was about to refuse Muro's request, but then he thought about how Vito Genovese and Carlo Gambino brought two zits over from Sicily to kill Anastasia, who, at the time, was the boss of Murder Incorporated. The two men killed him on October 25, 1957 while he was in the barber's chair at the Park Sheraton Hotel's barber shop, at 56th Street and 7th Avenue in Midtown Manhattan. Maybe those two men could be useful to him, he thought. "Think carefully before answering. Can I depend on him, Muro?"

"Yes, Red, you can depend on him."

"But can I trust him?"

"He's been my friend for years, and we've backed one another when we were in tight spots, and he's proven himself to me, so yes. I trust him."

"I'll take him with us, but if he betrays my trust, I'll kill him, and then I'll kill you. So be very careful in asking me to take him with us. Understand this. You are sponsoring him. If he fucks up, I'll blame you for it, and you'll pay along with him. Tomasso's life is in your hands, and yours in his. But with that aside, I'm willing to give you both the chance to prove yourselves, so consider your first year with me a probationary period."

"I'll talk to Tomasso tonight and I'll let him know your generous offer. Tomorrow, before we go to see Enzo, I'll tell you if he's coming with us, and I'll fill you in on what we thought was the best way to handle Enzo."

The Sicilian Caper

Red's Sicilian was getting better the more he used it. He wasn't using complete sentences yet, but he was using phrases. The language he heard his parents speak was coming back to him. He began speaking to Tarzan in Sicilian, so the language would become easier for him. After arranging things with Mario and Muro, Red and Tarzan left Mario's tobacco shop and returned to Sophia's home. Red was eager to see how Joey Boy was coming along. Sophia had a meal waiting for the men, which both men appreciated. But before Red sat down to eat his dinner, he stepped into Sophia's bedroom to see how Joey Boy felt. It surprised him to see him up watching Italian television. "You understand what they're saying, Joey?"

"Not a word, Red, but it beats sitting here twiddling my thumbs."

Red laughed. It was good to hear Joey Boy cracking jokes. "How are you feeling, Joey?"

"Much better today, Red. I feel myself getting stronger every day, and I'll tell ya Red, that gal is looking better to me every day. You know... When we leave here, I'm gonna miss her."

"You're not falling for her, are you, Joey?"

"You know, Red... I think I am. The gal is drop-dead gorgeous. She's beautiful, and on top of that, she's smart as hell. How could I not fall for her?"

"Well, get over it, because we'll be leaving soon."

"Maybe I'll stay a while longer, Red."

"I wouldn't do that, Joey. It's shortly going to get hot here, and you may have a problem explaining how you got your gunshot wounds."

"Maybe we could take Sophia with us, Red?"

"She's going to go back to medical school in Italy soon, and she won't have time to tend to you."

"Let's ask her if she would like to come to America with us. She can continue her education and go to medical school in New York City."

"That's still a big no, Joey Boy. She stays here. But you have my permission to visit her in Sicily whenever you want."

Joey Boy hung his head. "Aww, Red," he mumbled as he slowly shuffled back to the bedroom, lost in his thoughts. Red watched him walk away, and he saw the improvement in Joey's health. He was healing fast, and shortly, he'd be ready to join Red and the men, but in order for that to happen, he needed to continue healing, but it wouldn't be long now, Red thought.

"Did you speak to your friend Tomasso last night, Muro?"

"Yes, he guards Enzo during daylight hours and he goes home when it gets dark. Enzo figures no one could find their way through the maze of trees and shrubbery at night, so knowing that Tomasso wouldn't agree to be a prisoner of Enzo's so to relieve the pressure on Tomasso, Enzo allowed him to go home at night, so long as he was back at the break of dawn."

"So what did he say, Muro?"

"He told me he would do anything to be on the plane with me. I told him to call in sick, but he refused and came up with a better solution. He would tell Enzo that I spotted strangers, and I wanted to talk to him about them. He told Enno I had their descriptions, and where they were staying, and I wanted to discuss what to do in person with Enzo, and he agreed."

"How do we get up there? Do we use mules or horses, or do we hike up to the cave?" Red asked.

"Horses are the best way to get to the cave. It's faster to use a horse to get up the mountain. Of course, you can walk up the mountain to get to the cave, but it is very tiring. You'd be exhausted by the time you reached the cave. The problem is Mario has two horses. We can go to the blacksmith's and rent two more horses from him, but why Mario would want to rent two more horses would raise suspicions."

"So, how do you suggest we go up the mountain?" Red asked again.

"I'll ride double on one horse, and we'll use my two horses to bring two of you up the mountain. We'll drop two men off and then I'll take the two horses back down the mountain and we'll take two more men up, but on the way up, I'll ride double on the other horse so as not to tire one horse more than necessary. It wouldn't be a problem for the horses if we were on level ground, but a horse tires when it carries two men up the mountain."

Red was a brilliant tactician, having had to make life and

death decisions while running one of the largest mobs in America. "Make the first trip & drop two men off, then go back, change horses, and make a second trip. That'll be all that would be required. We'll deal with Enzo and walk back down the mountain. On the first trip, you'll take me and Muro, the second trip take Tarzan, and Pissclam. Got it, Mario?"

"Yes. I got it." Red chuckled at Mario's use of American slang.

"So, what are we waiting for? Get the horses and let's head up that mountain," Red told Mario.

CHAPTER 16

Mario used his two horses, and he dropped off Red and Muro about a hundred feet from the cave where they wouldn't see the two men. Mario turned his reins and walked the horses back down the mountain to get Tarzan and Pissclam. He'd been gone for thirty minutes, when Red had become restless. Red was eager to find Enzo and deal with him. He relaxed when he saw two horses struggling up the trail, with one horse carrying two men. When they got to where Red stood waiting, Tarzan slid off his horse. "Whew, that was some ride," Tarzan said, wiping his brow.

"Come on, Muro, let's get this over with. I don't want Enzo slipping away from me again. This guy is one pain in the ass, and I want him silenced forever, so show me where his cave is." The men followed Muro and climbed the short distance to a ledge hidden by foliage that snaked around the mountain.

"There are caves in this mountain that were used as a refuge by animals and man alike, but Enzo discovered a cave that is impossible to see unless you are right on top of it, and even then you would pass right by it if you didn't know it was there. Come, it's not far, and you will see what I am talking about for yourself." The men walked along the narrow shelf until Muro put his hand out to stop them. "The cave is just past that bend, so be quiet. Tomasso knows we are coming, and when he gets my signal, he will conveniently answer nature's call." Muro tapped a key on his walkie talkie and waited. His walkie talkie beeped twice, letting him know Tomasso received his signal and Enzo would be alone in the cave for the next twenty minutes. "Come, we must hurry, before Enzo becomes suspicious." The men reached the cave and the way the

The Sicilian Caper

mountain hid the cave impressed Red. Muro yelled, "Hello the cave. It's me, Muro."

Enzo relaxed. "Come on in, Muro. Tomasso will return in a few minutes." Muro walked through the crevice and into the cave. Red was right behind him, but Enzo saw only Muro and he relaxed. "Tomasso told me you saw strangers. What did you find out about them?"

Red stepped forward, his gun pointing at the unarmed Enzo. "He found out that Big Red Fortunato is here, and he wants revenge for you killing his father and robbing his bookmakers and trucks." Fear tentacles wrapped themselves around Enzo, and for the first time in his life, he discovered what fear really was. He turned paste white, and he trembled uncontrollably. "The law of the vendetta, Enzo. You're a Sicilian, and you act surprised to see me? Shame on you. I thought you were a tough guy, and here you are trembling like a scared little girl."

Tarzan and Pissclam stepped into the cave with their guns pointing straight at Enzo. Enzo was trapped, and he knew it. There would be no reprieve for him, but having no other choice, he tried to reason with Red. "It was an accident, Red. Surely you can see that. We were told our target was in a restaurant having dinner with a friend. We had no way of knowing our target couldn't make dinner because of his getting into a traffic accident on the way to the restaurant. Two other men sat at that table, so we had no way of knowing they weren't the men they sent us to kill. I discovered our mistake when it was too late. I knew you and Vito wouldn't understand and they would place a contract on me, so I had no choice but to run. Through the years, I became bitter, because I made an honest mistake and because of that I had to go on the run for all these many years. Let me go, Red, and I promise I'll never be a problem to you again."

Red nodded unemotionally. "I know you mean what you say, Enzo, and although I appreciate everything you just told me, my father is still dead, murdered by you." Red pulled the trigger twice and two bullets hit Enzo in his chest, knocking him off of his feet, crashing backwards against the mountain's hard, unyielding stone wall. Red walked over to the body and emptied his gun into Enzo's face and head, leaving Enzo unrecognizable.

"Throw this piece of shit down the mountain. The animals have to eat too." Red handed his gun to Pissclam. "Now there is one," he said with a bitter smile on his lips, and for a moment, Mario thought it was him he was talking about. "Tomorrow, after we kill Don Castillo, we'll be free to go home.

Red and his men bumped into Tomasso when they left Enzo's cave. Tomasso watched Pissclam and Tarzan throw Enzo's body off the mountain, and he knew these men were as deadly as the mafiosos he worked for. He caught Red's eye, not knowing if Red would take him with them to America, or kill him like he killed Enzo. He held his breath as Red approached him. "You kept your word, and for that, I'm gratified. Go home and pack a suitcase. You're coming to New York with us. You and Muro will work for me from now on. But before we can leave Sicily, I have one more piece of business to take care of, and I expect to finish that piece of business tomorrow. Then we'll be free to leave Sicily." Red looked around the dimly lit cave. "Search the place. This bum stole a lot of money from me, and some of it may still be here."

The men searched Enzo's living area of the cave and found nothing of value. "We found nothing, Red."

Red scratched his three days' growth of beard, while looking into the darkness beyond Enzo's living quarters. "Get a torch and look at the rear of the cave. He may have hid his money or something valuable back there." Muro had a flashlight, so Tarzan took Enzo's flashlight, knowing he wouldn't need it any longer. They began a slow, thorough search, beginning in the rear section of the cave. They discovered the cave was much larger than they first thought, and it extended much further back than they realized.

Red ordered them to search only the area of the cave that extended beyond the part Enzo used. They found nothing, but as Pissclam was walking back to where Red waited, he noticed a stone slab that was slightly off kilter. It wasn't lying flat on the stone it lay upon. It took effort on Pissclam's part, but he pushed the slab forward so it eased off the stone base, and his eyes lit up. "Hey, Red. Come back here. I found something interesting."

Red walked over to Pissclam. "What did you find,

The Sicilian Caper

Pissclam?"

"Look for yourself, boss."

Red looked into the open cavity and was speechless. "Pissclam, you really hit the jackpot." Inside the stone cavity were stacks of one-hundred-dollar bills wrapped in cellophane. "This is the money Enzo got from robbing my bookmakers and trucks. We'll count it later at Sophia's place. Check the other slabs, and you might find some of the smaller stolen items he couldn't fence, or sell. Pissclam found one stash, and I'll bet there are other stashes hidden back there, and if you find anything, I bet it'll be something expensive, because every truck Enzo robbed contained expensive items."

Having found one stash, the men began searching for another hoard of stolen items. It didn't take long before Pissclam found a stash of fur coats in a cutout in the wall. The coats were each carefully wrapped in a protective plastic sleeve. Red shook his head. *How the hell did that resourceful punk Enzo get the fur coats to Sicily, and through customs? Well, he had nothing else to do and being up here all alone in his cave, he had all the time in the world to wrap the furs without fear of being disturbed by anyone,* he said to himself.

"Let's rig a travois to pack the furs on, and we'll take the horses down to Mario's store and leave them tied to the rail. Then we'll drop the furs off at Sophia's place. She can hand them out to her neighbors. Besides being stylish, the coats will keep the ladies warm in the winter." They stacked the furs on the travois, and Red watched the last strap being tied to the travois. "Pissclam will carry the cash we found, and since there's nothing else to take, we're finished here. Let's head back down the mountain."

Red tied his horse to the hitch rail in front of the tobacco shop and walked in. Mario looked at Red expectantly, and with sad eyes, he knew Enzo wasn't leaving the mountain. Red just nodded, and Mario understood. He was sad that his cousin Enzo was dead, but he knew one day it had to happen. Enzo was a bad seed, always looking to take something from someone, or just hurt someone for little or no reason. Still... Enzo was his first cousin. He was family, and he was used to him coming into his store and taking a half dozen cigars and not paying for them, even though he always had plenty of money in his pocket. That was why Enzo surprised him when he came back from his recent trip to America, and he gave him money to buy gifts for his wife and children. Enzo was unpredictable, and Mario thought he had a touch of craziness in him because of the way he acted. One day he would act perfectly normal, and the next day he was like a crazy man capable of killing anyone who aggravated him. He was a ruthless killer and Mario knew it, and that was why he didn't feel any remorse when Red told him Enzo would no longer visit him in his cigar store… he was dead.

"Pissclam."

"Yes boss."

"Get one of the fur coats and give it to Mario for his wife. Then bring the car around the back of the store. Toot the horn and I'll meet you at the back of the store by the door. I'll have the fur coats ready to load into the car, so pull up close to the back door."

Pissclam tooted the horn and Red opened the back door and together they loaded as many fur coats as they could in the back seat and the trunk, as there wasn't enough room to fit all the coats in the car. A second trip was necessary. "Take the fur coat, Mario, and give it to your wife. She deserves it."

Mario was speechless. "Thank you, Red. My wife will love the coat. She's never had a coat like this one, because I could never afford such an expensive coat."

"Well now she has one. Make sure she gets it."

"I will, Red, and thank you for thinking of me."

"What's in the boxes, Red?" Sophia asked.

"It's a surprise for you and the women in Gratteri." Red saw the confused expression on Sophia's face. "Open a box. You might like what's in it," Red said.

She opened a box out of curiosity, but when she saw what was in the box, she knew she had to have one of the luxurious fur coats. "Oh, Red. How much would one coat cost me?"

He smiled at her. "You can't afford one of these coats." Her face dropped, showing her disappointment. "Don't look so disappointed, Sophia. I said you couldn't afford one of these coats, but you can have any coat you want for nothing. In fact,

The Sicilian Caper

I want this Christmas to be something special for the women in Gratteri. You're going to be in charge of making sure every woman in this town gets a free fur coat. It'll be our Christmas present to all the women in Gratteri, so tell me, are you up for doing this for me?"

"Oh, Red," she cried and ran and put her arms around him.

"Hey, what's going on here." Joey Boy said, smiling. "What are you doing hugging my girl, Red?"

Red gave Joey Boy a tight-lipped smile. "I got carried away thinking of how happy all the women in Gratteri will be when they get an expensive fur coat for free from Sophia next Christmas. Go on, Sophia, go through the rest of the boxes and check out the other fur coats. If you see another coat you like, put it aside and keep it for yourself."

She looked up at Red. "Red, just how many coats did you bring here?"

"I figure there are enough fur coats to give one to every woman in Gratteri, but next Christmas, that'll be your job. It'll be up to you to make sure every woman in Gratteri gets a fur coat for Christmas. If there are not enough coats for every woman, then hold a raffle, and give the coats out to the winners until the coats run out. That's fair, isn't it?"

"Yes, that's very fair, and I will get started on making a list of all the women in Gratteri, right after you men have left for America, and I'm alone."

"That works for me," Red said, happy now that they had settled the fur coat problem. Now the coats would be Sophia's problem, but when he looked at it from her point of view, it was a pretty pleasant problem for a young lady to have. Now that they took care of the coats, he could turn his attention to getting into the castle and then find Don Castillo and fix his sorry ass once and for all. But before Red could do that, he needed intelligence. How many men would Castillo have in the castle with him, and what room or hallway did the secret tunnel open up to? Were there any surprises he should know about before confronting Castillo? He'd ask Mario, and if he couldn't answer his questions, then Red would have to pay another visit to Dominick at the old people's home.

Mario couldn't answer Red's questions, so having no other

Joe Corso

choice, they drove to the retirement home, and instead of stopping at the desk, they walked up the stairs directly to Dominick's room. The room was empty, but they spotted the wheelchair outside on the veranda where they found him last time they visited him. Red thought Dominick was sleeping, but when they approached him, he looked at them and smiled. "I hope that package you're holding are the cigars you promised to bring me."

Red laughed. "I guess I can't hide anything from those sharp eyes of yours."

"You have that right, young fella. Now hand me a cigar and let's you and me have a smoke, but wheel me out of sight of my prison guards."

"They're not prison guards. They're just trying to keep you around to see another birthday."

"At my age, all I want to do is enjoy what little time I have left, and smoking a cigar once a day won't hurt me," Dominick said, lighting his cigar.

"Pass me the lighter, Dominick," Red asked.

The old man's sharp eyes assessed Red. "Now I know you didn't come here just to bring me the box of cigars, so what brought you here?"

"I have a few questions to ask you about the cave and Castillo's castle."

"I told you what I knew the last time you were here, but ask your questions. Maybe I can answer them for you."

"What do you know about the traps in the tunnel?"

"The traps were designed by old time engineers, and they were good at their job. I learned about them from Don Castillo's grandfather's father, who was told about it by his grandfather, so I'll share the little I was told about them with you. The old man told me they built the first trap near to the entrance. If an intruder stepped on the wrong flat stone that was built into the floor of the cave, it would release a series of large bolt like arrows, or small harpoons from the walls on either side of the cave. The intent of the engineers was to ensure that they killed the intruders. I don't know how they secured the arrows or bolts inside the walls and disguised them so the person walking past them couldn't see them. You had better hope the tension bars securing the bolts in place no longer have tension on them and whatever material they used to propel the arrows are no longer functional, but my guess is they took that possibility into account."

"What about the second trap? What do you know about that one?"

"When, or I should say… if you get past the first trap, keep to the side of the cave, staying close to the walls. They built the second trap to release tons of stone boulders to come crashing down on the intruders, killing them instantly."

"And the third trap?" Red asked.

"Ahh, the third trap is the most fiendish of them all. The old Don told me the third trap has many poison-tipped darts embedded in the walls on both sides of the cave. I do not know if the poison is still effective, but why take any chances? You must avoid them at all costs."

"How can we do that?" Red asked, his face showing concern.

"To avoid the darts would be difficult, and when he was alive, the old Don and me talked about this problem for hours. He never figured on using the cave's escape route in case they attacked the castle."

"And what did you two come up with?"

"The old Don suggested we make several round, light, protective metal can-like objects with hinges built on one side so it can open and a person can step inside of it and wrap it around themselves, lock it, and then proceed carefully past the trap containing the poison darts. He told me his grandfather gave him that idea. He said his grandfather told him the original engineers came up with that idea."

"Were any ever built?" Red asked.

"I was told that they had built a few, but were never used."

"Where exactly are the traps located?"

"Bring me your map of the cave area. I want to look at it."

Red opened his attaché case and took out the map and handed it to the old man. "Bring the light closer to me. I don't see well these days." The sun was shining brightly, but Red handed the old man a flashlight he took from his attaché case. The old man studied the map, and then he pointed to a section of the cave. "Here, mark this as the location of the first trap." He waited while Red made notes on the border of the map near the first trap, mentioning what the danger was they should know. The old man held the flashlight, searching for the spot on the map where the second trap was located. "Here! Mark this area as the second trap, and write on the edge what the trap is." Red wrote notes concerning the second trap on the margin. The old man took the map and studied what Red wrote in the margins, then apparently agreeing with what Red had written in the margins, studied the section of the map where the third trap should be located. He was pretty sure of the trap locations, but after so many years, how could anyone be sure of his memory or the map's accuracy? "Here. This is where the third trap should be located."

Red's eyes widened. "Should be located? I thought you knew where the traps were actually located?"

"Mr. Red, after so many years of never seeing this map or thinking about the traps built into the cave's entrance, how can anyone, even if they built the traps, remember their exact locations? Even though I can't give you the exact locations of the traps, the information I'm giving you will save your life, and the lives of your friends, but you must pay close attention to the information I'm sharing with you."

"You told me there were four traps. What about the fourth trap? What kind of trap is it and where is it located?"

"The old Don told me that the fourth trap was an afterthought. He wanted one more measure of protection, just in case intruders got past the first three traps." The old man brought the map close to his face so he could see it better, because even with his thick prescription glasses, his eyesight wasn't very good. "Come closer, young man, and listen to me carefully. The fourth trap is located here," he said, pointing to the map and then to the entrance into the castle at the very top of the cave. "You must be careful, because if you push the wrong stone, the bottom will fall from under your feet. You can see how the cave developed during the eons of time it existed. Not only did the cave escape route form, but waters from prehistoric times cut areas below that route away. The fourth trap uses the area below the cave's escape route to kill all

The Sicilian Caper

intruders who made it past the first three traps."

Red didn't like what the old man just told him about the four traps. Back in Queens, there was nothing he couldn't handle. He feared no one and backed down to no one, and if anyone threatened him, he would deal with that person. But here in the ass-end of Sicily, he knew nothing of caves, and secret passages, and traps constructed centuries ago in what Red referred to as the archives of time. He understood the streets, but he didn't understand a person like Enzo who lived in a cave, nor opening a hidden, locked entrance to a cave leading into a medieval castle. He was claustrophobic in confined areas, specifically old caves. Just the thought of him going into that old cave made him feel uncomfortable, and out of his comfort zone, but he'd keep his feelings to himself, and he'd open the damn entrance to the cave, and he would challenge the four traps one trap at a time while he climbed the interior of the mountain to the entrance into the castle at the very top of the cave's escape route.

Red took out his handkerchief and wiped his brow. "I'm about two minutes from calling this whole thing off. It's getting a little complicated for this city boy."

The old man chuckled. "I thought you were a tougha guy, but it looks to me as if you are a frightened little pussy." Red would kill a person who insulted him, like the old man just did, and the old man must have seen the reaction on Red's face after he said that to him. "Come closer, young man." Although Red was pissed off at the old man, he moved closer to him. "Listen to me. There's nothing to be afraid of in that cave but the traps. I've given you all the information you need to understand and avoid the traps. If you kill that bastardo Don Castillo, you will be a hero to the people who have lived their whole life in fear in Gratteri. Do it and don't be afraid of the unknown. Open the cave and defeat each trap as you get to it. And then go find the Don. It'll take you twenty or thirty minutes, maybe longer if you go slow, but something just occurred to me, the old Don warned me that once you get to the top, there's a peephole in a brick at the entrance. Pull it aside and look in the room. The old timers put it there so they wouldn't open the secret door and walk into a room full of people. When you reach the top of the

133

escape route, the entrance into the castle is a lever to the right of the peephole, but remember to look through the peephole first. Look into the room to make sure the room is empty before opening the secret door."

Upon hearing this last piece of important information the old man just told him, Red felt better. He calmed down, and his anger abated, and while he still dreaded entering that old cave, his desire to get back at Castillo for attempting to kill him and his men balanced his feelings. They ambushed and killed Tic-Tok at Mario's tobacco shop, and for that alone, Don Castillo gave up his life.

Mario drove Red back to Sophia's home, and Red wasted no time in calling his men to a meeting in the living room. Joey Boy shuffled in to attend the meeting, even though Red wouldn't use him when they opened the entrance to the cave leading up to Castillo's castle. Red spread the map of the cave's emergency exit down through the cave's labyrinth, leading down to the locked gate blocking the entrance to the cave's interior. "This is how we're entering the cave. Through the locked gate, a gate they locked over two centuries ago, but I have the key to open that lock. We'll have to bring a can of lubricating oil with us, because that lock hasn't been opened in a long, long time. We'll have to take a tool that can cut through metal just in case we can't get the lock to open with the key I dug up, according to Dominick's instructions."

"Who's Dominick?" Pissclam asked.

"He used to work for Castillo's grandfather. Dominick is one hundred and one years old and he used to be head of security for the old Don. He's the one who filled me in on how to get in the gate, and he told me about the traps incorporated into the design of the escape route, using the cave to escape from the danger of an attack by a neighboring principality. When we get the gate open, we'll have to be very careful. We don't want to accidentally trigger a trap, and there are four traps to watch out for." For the next two hours, Red discussed each of the four traps individually. Red showed the men the large two-hundred-year-old key.

"Man, talk about a phallic symbol," Pissclam said, causing the men to chuckle. "Did you see the gate, boss?"

The Sicilian Caper

"Yes, I did. The gate is ancient, so we'll try the key first, and if it doesn't open the lock, we'll use acetylene, and cut the lock off or use it to open the gate. Either works for me."

"What about the traps, Red? What were you told about them?" Tarzan asked. Red explained all he knew about the traps. He explained where each trap was located, and what damage the trap could do to the person who triggered one of the four traps. Red warned his men of the danger that ran throughout the cave's escape route. He could see each man felt as he did. The men weren't used to a fight like this. Like Red, they were used to taking the fight to the men of the street who posed a threat to them, but entering a cave that was locked closed for over two hundred years was something else. They weren't used to this kind of fight, and not only that, they were used to facing men with guns or fists. Not stepping on a stone and getting skewered. That wasn't their kind of fight. A fight where they couldn't even get a punch, or a shot in, and that caused the men to have second thoughts about going into that dangerous cave, and they told Red how they felt.

"Look, fellas. I'll be the first one in that cave, and I feel the same way you do, but I'll still be the first one in there."

"I'll be right behind you, Red," Trenchie said.

"Me too," Tarzan echoed.

"I guess you can count me in too, Red," Pissclam said.

"That's what I want to hear. Look, we can be up that path in less time than you think. I want to get that Castillo bastard, and he won't be expecting us to come after him through a gate that's been closed for over two centuries."

Trenchie swept his arm in a wide arc. "If these chicken-shit bastards are afraid to come with us, they can wait outside for us, and watch how real men handle this joker." Trenchie shamed the rest of the men into joining them.

"Okay then. We'll start early tomorrow morning, right after breakfast. Is everyone on board? Let's see a show of hands."

All the men raised their hands. "Tomorrow, right after breakfast, we'll drive to the cave's entrance. Pissclam, talk to Mario and make sure we take an acetylene tank and torch with us, just in case the lock is so rusted the key won't work. And bring a can of lubricating oil to loosen the lock up. I want every one of you armed, and bring a flashlight with fresh batteries with you. If we have to before we leave town, we'll stop at a store to get the batteries."

"I have a can of lubricating oil," Sophia, standing in the doorway, said.

"Sophia, while I finish my meeting with my men, get the can of lubricating oil."

When the meeting ended, the men knew what they would face when they opened the entrance and entered the cave.

When Red finished talking to his men, he turned, and it pleased him to see Sophia standing there holding the can of lubricating oil.

"I'll bring this can of oil back to you tomorrow when we return from the castle. Come on, Pissclam, we're taking a brief ride."

"Where are we going, boss?"

"We're taking a ride to the entrance to the cave. I want to squirt oil into the lock and let it set for the night, so when we get there in the morning, the lock should open." At least Red hoped the lock would open without a problem.

The Sicilian Caper

CHAPTER 17

At 6 am the following morning, Red, Tarzan, Pissclam, Ron Sal, Muro, Tomasso were at the cave. Captain Frankie, the pilot, had asked Red to include him in anything they were planning. Frankie told Red it bored him just hanging around the terminal, and he wanted to be a part of whatever they were planning, so he was there too. Red, with his paranoia when speaking on the telephone, didn't want to say too much, just in case ears were listening in on their conversation. So he gave Frankie Sophia's address, and he told him he'd explain everything to him when he got to the house. That was last night. This morning, he was a part of the crew that was about to break into a cave that was used as an escape route two centuries ago by the local prince. They had sealed the escape route through the cave since then.

Red took the key he found in the metal box. He had followed Dominick's directions and dug the box up ten paces behind the nearest tree in front of the locked gate . He inserted the ancient key into the lock and turned it. At first, the lock resisted the key's attempt to turn the tumblers after so many years of stagnation and rusting, but to Red's surprise, at the second try, the resistance disappeared, and the lock turned. "I guess the lubricating oil worked. Now let's see if it also worked on the gate's hinges," he said to himself. The gate resisted once again, and this time, it took three grown men pulling hard and tugging, and pulling some more until the stubborn gate broke free and its oiled hinges swung loosely. "Pissclam, pull the car into that copse of trees and make sure it's well hidden. Place a lot of loose branches over the car so no one sees it. I don't want anyone to know what we're up to. Understand? When you've hidden the car, join us inside the opening. We'll wait for you inside the gate, so hurry. Don't keep us waiting. And make sure no one sees you entering the castle through the gate, understand?"

"No one will walk around here at 6 am, boss, it's too early, but in case someone does walk by, I'll be careful and make sure they don't see me." Pissclam drove the car into the copse of trees Red had pointed to, and he added branches and a heavily leafed branch that a lightning strike had hit and cut cleanly from the tree. Pissclam used that branch to hide the rest of the car. Satisfied that a passing car or a pedestrian walking his dog wouldn't notice the car, he rushed back to the open gate, closed it behind him, making sure not to lock it, and he rushed into the cave's entrance.

"Okay, let's go, but remember the traps, and be careful not to trigger any." Red pulled the map out and looked at where the first trap was situated. He studied the map and then he turned his attention to his surroundings, and he studied the walls, and that was when he spotted the small round holes built into the walls on either side of the cave. Dominick said they would trigger the bolts when someone stepped on one particular stone, the stone that would trigger the mechanism that would release the deadly bolts. Red reasoned that logic would suggest the stone would have to be larger than the others, because the designers of the trap wouldn't chance the stone not being stepped on, because the stone was too small, and was unintentionally stepped over, not triggering the bolts. *No... If it were me installing this trap, I'd make sure the stone was large enough so a person couldn't miss stepping on the stone. But wait a minute,* Red thought. No matter how large the stone was, an intruder might still step around it, and if that were the case, then the original builders might consider installing a series of large stones, which would guarantee the intruders couldn't help but step on the triggering stone. "Hold it, guys. Don't take another step until I assess the situation. Look at the floor for a long, flat slab. I'm betting that's the triggering mechanism, and if you were to stop on it, those bolts or arrows would skewer you. Pissclam, pick up that large rock over there in the corner, and throw it so it lands on that long, flat slab." Pissclam picked up the stone Red pointed to and threw it, and when it landed on the flat slab, it detonated an explosion of what appeared to be hundreds of bolts shooting out from the round holes in the walls on both sides of the cave. "Hell, if I didn't see this for myself, I wouldn't believe it. Those old engineers knew how to build a trap, and that's for sure... and it still worked over two hundred years after they installed it. Amazing. We've got three more traps to be wary of, so listen to what I tell you and don't get careless... or stupid," Red admonished.

"What do we do about the second trap, boss?" Pissclam asked Red.

"The old man told me if something triggered the second trap, it released tons of stone boulders that will crash down from an overhead vault on the intruders, killing all of them instantly."

"That doesn't sound to encouraging, boss," Pissclam said with a tinge of worry in his tone of voice.

"You're right, Pissclam. It's not encouraging, so that means we have to be extra vigilant where and what we step onto. If I place myself in the mindset of the old engineers who designed and built the traps, I'd make it simple."

"Simple? How, boss?" Pissclam asked.

"Well, I'd build the same triggering mechanism for each trap. The results would be different, of course, but the means to set the trap off or trigger it would remain the same. Let's see if I'm right. Stay behind me, keep your flashlights on the floor in front of us, and let's move ahead slowly and carefully."

It appeared to the men that they were in a long tomb and they were venturing along a path with no exit, but they would follow Red into hell if that was where he was leading them. To the men following him, Red appeared to know the route the cave was taking them on, and his self-assurance gave the men the confidence that he knew exactly what he was doing. It took Red and the men following him longer than expected, because they examined every stone they had to step on to move forward up along the slanting path the cave took them on, until Red raised his hand to signal the men to halt behind him. "I'm looking for the same type of slab that triggered the first trap. Shine your lights, boys, and let's find that flat rock because we sure as hell don't want to step on it by accident and find ourselves buried under a ton of rocks. So let's take it one step at a time, and not make any mistakes that could cost us our lives." They moved ahead slowly, very slowly, looking down at every rock on the floor in front of them. After stepping slowly ahead for what seemed like an eternity, but was in reality only thirty minutes, Red spotted what he thought was the trigger rock slab. It appeared to be a long, flat piece of rock, but was suspiciously out of place among the smaller rocks surrounding it. As he walked interminably slowly forward, he thought to himself, *Give me the old days when you lined a guy up against the wall and just shot the hell out of him, not this slow walk into your tomb if you were unlucky enough to step on the wrong stone among the hundreds of stones covering the path upwards to the entrance to the castle.*

The usually stoic Tarzan had to admire how Red logically discovered how to spot the rocks or slabs that would trigger the traps, and traps were the right word to describe the horror of what waited for them if they unexpectedly triggered a trap. Red stopped the men once again. "I think I see the slab that'll trigger the second trap, but what I'm concerned about is where can we take shelter from the boulders that will rain down on us. Before we take another step forward, let's study our surroundings carefully. The old engineers must have thought of this problem. What if the builders accidentally triggered the trap? Where would they go to keep from being killed? Look around, guys, but be careful where you step."

Pissclam spotted the anomaly. "Hey, boss, what's in that dark area over there?" he said, pointing to a darkened area of the wall about fifteen feet from where the men stood.

"I don't know, Pissclam, but when we approach it, we'll check it out."

Red guided the men past the stone slab he believed was the stone that would trigger the trap, and after witnessing the destructive power of the first trap, he wasn't keen on seeing what the second trap would do when triggered. If the old engineer who designed this trap built a means for him and his men to take refuge in a safe place within their design, he hoped to find it, and if he did, he'd try to trigger the second trap, and be rid of the danger the trap in its present state represented. The next few steps brought the men closer to the shadowed, or

The Sicilian Caper

darkened, area that Pissclam had pointed to. Finally, they stood in front of the dark area, which proved to be an alcove recessed into the interior rocky shelf of this part of the mountain. Red shined his flashlight into the darkness, and then he slowly followed the light into the alcove. A few minutes later, the men followed Red into the darkness.

"Well, lookie here," Red said, pointing to four cylindrical objects. "It looks like we found our way to get past the third trap, which is the poison darts. Pissclam, look for another rock, heavy enough to trigger the second trap. When you find the right rock, be careful where you step when you carry it into the alcove."

A short while later, Pissclam came grunting into the darkness and plopped the rock down in front of Red. "Which stone do you want me to throw the rock on Red?"

Red pointed to the flat stone slab. "Throw the rock on that stone over there," he said, pointing to the stone he believed would trigger the second trap. "Step back, men. I don't know what's going to happen when we trigger the trap, but I don't want to take any chances. Okay, Pissclam throw the rock."

Pissclam flung the rock, and at first, nothing happened, and then a groaning sound permeated the entire cave. It was as if the mountain was waking up after a long sleep, and then all hell broke loose as an explosion ripped the ceiling and interrupted the silence in the cavernous interiors open area. Red knew they used gunpowder two hundred years ago, but he did not know if the gunpowder was still dry after all these many years, and he wondered what they used to trigger the gunpowder. While Red pondered these questions, the ceiling opened up, raining hundreds of boulders into the darkness below, right where the men would have been standing. The men waited until the boulders settled into a new formation and the danger had passed. "Come on, guys, let's see if we still have a way to get up to the top and into the castle." They stepped out of the alcove and onto a ledge. Red looked up and was pleased to see they still had a path to the top available to them.

Don Castillo felt the mountain rumble and dust issued from every crevice. "What the hell was that?" Paulo asked.

Paulo was Don Castillo's primary bodyguard, and he remained with Castillo all day and accompanied him wherever he went.

"Some fool probably found the entrance into the mountain and decided to explore the cave, and all the fool bought was his death."

"I never knew there was an entrance to the mountain."

"There was no reason for you to know, Paulo. It has been closed for over two hundred years, and that fool found out why it has been closed. It has traps built into it, traps that would curl your hair. No man in his right mind would ever enter that cave knowing the traps he had to get past. No one, not even I, knows what type of traps are built into the mountain, and to be perfectly honest with you, I don't ever want to know."

"Should I go investigate?"

"Nah, why bother. If a fool set off that trap, then he's a dead fool. No one could have survived after triggering a trap."

Red pointed to the rusting circular structures. "You two," Red said, pointing to Pissclam and Sal. "Try on one of those contraptions. If it fits, take it with you, and we'll try it out on the third traps poison darts."

"Wait a minute, boss. I didn't volunteer for this," Pissclam said.

"You can relax, Pissclam, I just volunteered for you."

"Oh?" Pissclam said, wondering what just happened.

So far, the old traps were working, which surprised Red. Two hundred years rotting away in a cold, damp environment, and the traps still functioned. *Amazing*, Red thought. So far he brought his men past two functioning traps. He still had two more traps to get past, but the bright side was, he was more than halfway to his goal. Now he had to get past the final two traps alive. He pondered this while waiting for Pissclam and Sal to settle in the round metal contraptions. "What's it like in there, Pissclam?"

"Pretty clever, boss. The metal is framed around wood, and there's handles built into the wood so the person inside can lift the cage to move it."

"Is that contraption heavy?" Red asked

The Sicilian Caper

"Yeah, it is. I guess they built these metal cages just to move it a few feet in order to trigger the third trap, but I wouldn't want to wear this thing from the opening at the gated entrance where we came in, up to the very end at the top." Red knew he had to keep a clear head, but as he moved forward, he kept asking himself, *What the hell am I doing here. Enzo is dead, and that's what I came to Sicily to do... to kill Enzo. Hell I better finish this quick, before I throw up my hands and head back to Queens, where it's safe.* Red heard the clanking before he saw the two men half dragging, half carrying the oval shaped rusting metal contraptions. "Over here, guys," Red said, waving the two men forward to take positions in front of Red.

"Boss, are you sure you want us to do this?"

"Look, Pissclam. The old engineers must have had field tests using the darts against the metal containers, and since we found the containers in this cave, we have to assume that the old engineers, after testing the metal containers against the darts, discovered it would stop the poison darts, without killing the person inside the cage."

CHAPTER 18

Red moved slowly forward, keeping behind the two men navigating in front of him in the metal containers. His men kept pace close behind him. "Shine your lights on the walls and look for round cuts in the stone. That's where they would store the poisoned tipped darts until someone or something released them. For all we know, the darts may still be in those holes waiting to be released, and we assume that the scenario I just laid out for you is real, and the darts are still there waiting to be released, and that is where you two come in," Red said, pointing to the two cylindrical rusting metal objects with Pissclam and Sal inside of them. Tap twice if you understood what I just said, fellas."

A TAP - TAP, in response to Red's question, emanated from each cylindrical cage. Pissclam and Sal took the lead, knowing what their job was. Their steps were agonizingly slow, but they persisted, shuffling step by step slowly ahead. Red held the rest of the men in place behind him, allowing for the distance to be maintained between his two forward tank men, as he and the rest of his men now referred to Pissclam and Sal. Having allowed his two forward tank men to open the gap between them, he was about to move forward, when suddenly, hundreds of darts shot out of the walls on both sides of the cave and skewered, clattered, bounced, and flew off, the protective metal cylinders bouncing harmlessly to the rocky floor of the cave. "Okay, Pissclam, and you too, Sal, you can climb out of your metal suits. The danger is past, and you guys did great." Red turned to say a few words to the rest of his men. "Guys, the worst is over. We have one more trap to overcome, and then we're home free with no other obstacles to prevent us from

The Sicilian Caper

entering the castle. Now let's finish this job." Red took a moment to study the far wall. He figured there must be a narrow channel carved out of the mountain from thousands of years of water from the melting mountain snow, and that was what the old engineers discovered that enabled them to install the traps in the old castle. He was sure of one thing, and that was he had no interest in investigating that area of the mountain.

The grade steepened and walking uphill suddenly became tiring. Rocks and boulders of all sizes blocked the path to the top, but Red and his men were eager to finish this challenge, so they persisted in their attempt to reach the top, knowing they still had the fourth trap to encounter and overcome. "Listen up, men. When we reach the top, that's where the fourth trap is hiding. Press a wrong rock, or step on the wrong stone and the floor will open up under us, and we will disappear into the void below, never to be found alive again. So if you want to go home, let's get to the top and end this." The men wanted to reach the top knowing that would bring them that much closer to ending this nightmare. Once they reached the top, then it was a simple matter of timing before they could enter the castle. The climbing was slower at this point than while climbing toward the top, but there was a relaxed pace forward. It took longer than Red thought it would. The climb was arduous, unlike the first three-quarters of the climb. The last quarter was longer, steeper, and more difficult, with many more obstacles in their way.

But that was all in the past now that they had reached the top. Red was very careful where he stepped, fearful he might accidentally trigger the fourth and final trap... but maybe that last trap wouldn't have to be triggered, not if he was careful. He looked at his men milling about and he immediately raised a hand to put a stop to it.

"Listen up, guys. The less we move around, the better chance we have of not triggering the fourth trap. There is a stone either on the wall or on the ground that will trigger the fourth trap. I want you men to remain right where you are, and don't stray from that spot until I can find the means to get us into the castle. I'm going to stay as close to the castle wall as possible, and I don't want to see anyone behind me. I told you where I want you to stay, and I don't want to discover any of you disobeyed me. Listen to me and stay alive. If any of you trigger the fourth trap, the floor we're standing on will be hurled down into that great empty abyss below, taking us all with it," Red said, pointing to the empty void beckoning to them. He took a long last look to make sure his men remained where he told them to, and then he turned to the task at hand. He had to find the peephole, and when he found that, the old man told him the release was to the right of it.

Red searched each brick carefully, and then he found it. The brick had a built in metal slide, which was ingenious for its time, and rusted closed. He asked Pissclam for the penetrating oil and he squirted a generous amount onto the slide and he waited a few moments before trying to move it. Red pushed the slide hard, until it freed itself and slid smoothly. Red slid the metal slide to the left and put his eye on the opening, and he could see clearly into the room. He raised his hand and gave his men the thumbs-up. Now that he found the peephole, he slid his hand to the right to find the lever that would open the secret door. "Tarzan, come over here."

"What's up, Red."

"Keep looking through the peephole while I try to find the lever that will open the secret entrance into the castle."

Tarzan looked through the peephole and was impressed. "The old engineers knew what they were doing, Red. They did a great job on this peephole; it's great."

Red was about to answer Tarzan, but to the right of the peephole, his fingers felt something different. What was it the old man had said to him? *There is a lever to the right of the peephole. A lever. That's what I'm looking for, a lever.* He moved his fingers to the right of the peephole and he felt it again. He shined his light on the spot that felt different, and he was disappointed to find it was just another brick. Red moved his fingers forward along the same row of bricks as the peephole, but there was nothing different that he could find, so he slid his fingers back to the brick that felt different, and this time with a little patience, he discovered what he felt that was different about the brick. He found it wasn't a real brick at all, but a brick made of wood, and painted to look like brick. He pulled out his knife and scraped it along the face of the brick,

The Sicilian Caper

and in doing so, he pulled off the false front and saw that it had a hollow built inside of it. In the cut out hollow, he saw a recess carved into the interior of the false brick, with a metal lever snugged tightly into the carved hollow. When he reached his finger into the hollow, there was just enough room in the hollow for his finger to fit around the metal lever. "Tarzan?"

"Yes, Red."

"Look through the peephole and let me know if anyone is in the room. Is it empty?"

"The room is empty, Red."

"Good," Red said, pulling the lever up toward him. Two-centuries-old tumblers clicked into place and opened an inch, allowing the hidden door to slowly open. He motioned to his men to quietly follow him into the room, but he warned them to be careful of the stones they stepped on. Red went into the room first, followed by Tarzan, Pissclam, Ron, Sal, Muro, Tomasso, and last, Frankie the Pilot. Red took a long look around the room, and he liked what he saw. The room was sumptuous, belying the antiquity of the building. There was a crystal bar, with crystal glasses, a hanging crystal chandelier. Red tapestries lined the walls and an expensive, thick, sumptuous wall-to-wall white Turkish rug covered the entire floor. The sound of voices issuing from the hallway alerted the men that they were about to have company. "Relax," Red told his men. "We have the numbers, and we're the ones with the firepower. So keep your guns loaded and at the ready, and when they enter the room, we'll greet our hosts properly."

"Do you want me to shut the lights, boss?" Pissclam asked.

"No! Don't shut them, leave them on. The lights were on when we entered the room, so if the lights remain on, it won't raise any suspicions."

"Okay, boss."

The door opened and two men, deep in a conversation, entered the room. It took a moment before realization set in that there were men, many men in this room. The Don stood there gaping at the hard men holding guns pointed at him, and he could not mutter a word. No matter how hard he tried, the words wouldn't come. Red stifled a laugh because Castillo's lips moved, but nothing came out, and he looked like a fish out of water. "What's the matter? The cat got your tongue?" Red said with an easy smile.

"How... There is no way into this room. How, how did you get in here?"

"That's for us to know and for you to find out," Red said with the same amiable smile. He was actually enjoying this cat-and-mouse game, especially after the nerve-racking climb through the interior of the mountain that abutted the castle. The realization of what these men accomplished hit Castillo. "You men found the entrance to the cave, and you came through it and you made it past the four traps, and lived. No one could have possibly accomplished that. No one would have dared to try making it up the mountain and that's why the entrance had been locked for the last two hundred years." Talking about what these men accomplished was like a tonic to Castillo, and the more he talked and asked questions, the more relaxed he became, forgetting for the moment that these men did the impossible and overcame insurmountable odds, just for the opportunity to kill him, yet he pushed those thoughts aside, and thought only of what these men accomplished. Then his eyes drifted again to all the guns pointed at him, until Red's voice jarred him out of his reverie.

"Sit down, Castillo, and you take a seat too," he told Castillo's bodyguard; at least he thought he was Castillo's bodyguard. It was too bad the bodyguard was here, because when they killed Castillo, they'd have to kill him too. If they didn't, he would be a potential witness against Red and his men.

After overcoming his initial shock at seeing the number of strange men in his castle, Castillo regained his composure. "What exactly do you men want from me?" Castillo addressed his question to all the men, but he specifically directed it at Red.

"I will tell you why we're here and what I want from you. I came here to kill the man who murdered my father. Call it vendetta, call it revenge, call it anything you want, but I came here to kill Enzo, who has for years been nothing but a thorn in my side, and I wanted him dead."

"Well, did you get your wish?" Castillo said jovially.

"Yes, but you forgot one thing."

"Oh? And what is that?" Castillo asked.

The Sicilian Caper

"You killed one of my men and seriously wounded another. The man you wounded almost died from his wounds, but thankfully, he recovered."

Castillo smiled charmingly. "You also forget that you killed my men too, and you stole two other men of mine," he said, pointing to Muro and Tomasso.

"Yeah, well, now they're on my payroll, and you forgot something else."

"And please tell me, what else did I forget?"

"You forgot that in our world, you show respect to men of honor, even if they are from other countries. You forgot that, and that will cost you."

"Don't you dare to threaten me in my house."

Red's gaze bore down on Castillo without a hint of fear, which was something Castillo wasn't accustomed to. Everyone feared Don Castillo, except, it appeared, these stupido Americanos.

"I just insulted you. Now what are you going to do about it?" Red waited for a reply, but none came, so he pushed Castillo toward the couch.

"Get your hands off of me, and I won't sit there like I'm your lackey that you can order me around. Well, I won't do it. Not in my house, I won't."

"Sit down, and I'm not asking. I'm telling you," Red barked. Castillo stood his ground and refused to sit down until Red belted him once with a hard right hand to his mid-section, which doubled Don Castillo in half. Red then simply pushed him so he unceremoniously fell more than sat down on the couch. "There, that's better."

Red motioned to Pissclam to approach him.

"What's up, boss?"

"I want you to keep your eye on Castillo when I leave him." Red spoke to Pissclam knowing Castillo was listening, and he bet that while Don Castillo knew about the traps, he didn't know exactly what they were, and he wanted him to escape down the emergency escape route that the old engineers built for his ancestor. Red gave Pissclam a wink to let him know he wanted him to disregard his instructions and let the man step out the door, hoping he'd trigger the fourth trap that hadn't been set off yet, and knowing he could never make it down to the entrance. The entire route had collapsed onto itself. But Castillo had no way of knowing that.

Red continued to give Pissclam instructions. "Don't let him use the hidden door. If he bolts out of here through that secret door and makes his way down to the exit, we'll never get him."

Castillo had lived in this old castle all of his life, and he used this room, because it was his favorite room, and yet, he never knew there was a secret door hidden in plain sight. Castillo followed Red with his eyes. He watched him push a panel flush with the others on that wall. It was obvious to Castillo that the partition he pushed flush with the wall was the invisible door. Now he had to figure out how to open the door.

Pissclam followed the instructions Red had given him and pushed a panel on the wall and the hidden door opened a few inches, which was enough for him to throw his cigarette butt out through the opening. It showed Castillo where means to open the hidden door was. Castillo smiled as he thought of revenge. *You smug bastard, I'm going to have you gutted as soon as I can escape. I'll have to get out that door and then I'll work my way down the mountain to the gated opening and then I'll lose myself in the forest at the base of the mountain. Once I'm free, I'll return with enough men to kill Red and his men. This Americano bastardo doesn't know who he is reckoning with.*

The door opened, and Red stepped into the room and motioned to Pissclam. "Step outside with me a moment, Pissclam. There's something I have to tell you in private."

Good, Castillo thought. *The moment you two leave this room, I'll be out that hidden door and on my way to freedom.*

As soon as the door closed behind Pissclam, Castillo rushed to the hidden door and, after a few tries, found the means to open it. He rushed out of the room with his bodyguard close behind him into what they could have only described as hell. It looked to Castillo as if he had just stepped into an alternate universe and it gave him the chills. He was frozen in place for a long moment, but he knew he had to find his way down to the exit point, but there was no light other than the light from the still open secret hidden door. If he shut it, he'd be in pitch black

The Sicilian Caper

darkness without knowing how to reopen the hidden door. He noticed a flashlight on the brick shelf near the hidden door, and he reached for it, when suddenly, the floor under him disappeared, and he felt himself free falling into a black void of nothingness.

"Wow! Did you see that, boss?"

"Yeah, they were here one moment and gone the next. Well, good riddance to bad rubbish. The stupid bastard just saved us the trouble of having to whack him and his bodyguard. Now let's see what this castle has to offer. We'll start at the top and work our way down. I want every nook and cranny searched. I'd like the newly departed Don Castillo to pay for my new executive jet aircraft, so let's give this castle a thorough search. The way Castillo threw his money around, he must have a ready source of cash at his disposal, so let's see if we can find where he hid his hoard." They searched the top floor of the castle room by room. Castillo's bedroom was on the top floor, as well as his office. There was nothing of value in his bedroom other than the usual bedroom furniture, but they found a large safe in his office hidden behind a false wall. "I wish Ernie was here. I sure could use his safecracking talents now, but he's in Las Vegas and we're in Sicily in the little town of Gratteri."

Muro stepped forward. "If you'll permit me, Red. I have a little experience in dealing with safes, especially this type of safe."

"Why this type of safe, Muro?"

"Because I was the one that picked up the safe from the airport, and then when I brought it here, I set the safe up for Don Castillo."

"You wouldn't know the combination, would you?"

"I'll try using the original combination. If Don Castillo didn't change the combination, I should be able to open the safe." As a safecracker, Muro reminded Red of Ernie. They both were all business when opening a safe. Red figured they would have to be all business, because of the mental clarity he would need when he concentrated on each number of the combination and had to memorize the digits.

"Okay, let's try opening the door," Muro said as he turned the handle, and to his relief, the safe's door swung open.

Red looked in the safe but was disappointed when he didn't see the safe brim full of money. Instead, all he saw was paper, lots of paper, stacks of paper. He reached in and pulled out the wrapped stacks of paper and piled them neatly at the side of the large safe. He opened one of two drawers and lifted two canvas bags out, and laid them on the floor. The second drawer held deeds to many properties, including houses and businesses that Castillo owned. Even the deed to the castle was there. "The bastard must have foreclosed on the people who owned these properties," Red said. Yet he could understand it, because he did the same thing when someone owed him money and couldn't pay him. They paid him with the only thing of value they had, and that was their home or business.

As Red was sifting through the safe, Tarzan began looking through the bags of paper. "Red, stop what you're doing and look at this."

Red asked, "What did you find, Tarzan?"

"While you're looking for cash to pay for your new toy, I found these." He handed Red a few of the papers stacked against the side of the safe. Red took the paper Tarzan handed him and read it, and as he read the paper, his eyes widened. "Christ, do you know what these slips of paper are, Tarzan?"

"Of course I do. That's why I wanted you to look at them. They're bearer bonds cashable anywhere in the world."

"How many of these certificates are there?" Red asked.

"I'd say a couple of hundred, maybe more."

Red smiled. "That could pay for the plane, plus a bonus for each of the men." Then, almost as an afterthought, Red remembered the two canvas bags. "Open the canvas bags and let's see what Castillo was hiding among them. So far, I feel we're having an early Christmas, and we're about to have an even better New Year. Open the canvas bags, Tarzan."

CHAPTER 19

Tarzan opened the first canvas bag and sorted through the items in it, and then a luminous smile appeared on his face. "What's the smile for, Tarzan? Come on, spill it. Why the smile?" Red was antsy, wondering what Tarzan saw that caused him to smile.

Tarzan lifted the bag. "This canvas bag contains bank books from several banks, but from what I could determine, after sifting through the books, Castillo loaded the accounts with cash. The Don's been a busy man," Tarzan said, waving a bankbook at Red.

Red thought for a few minutes, and then said. "We're going to empty his bank accounts of all the cash. Have the men search the castle. Castillo must have several servants to cook for him and to clean and care for this place. I want to see all of them ASAP. Pissclam, get the car and drive over to Sophia's home and tell her I would like to see her at Don Castillo's castle, and then drive her back here."

"You want me to bring Joey Boy too, boss?"

"Sure. I miss Joey Boy. If he feels up to it, bring him here too, along with Sophia." Red motioned for the boys to follow him. "I want to search every room in this castle floor by floor, starting with this floor, and then we'll search the next floor and so on, until I know this castle like the back of my hand." The rooms on the top floor were sumptuous and couldn't be more luxurious even if the rooms were in a five-star hotel. They were on the fifth floor and they took the wide central staircase down to the fourth floor just as a group of servants were about to report to Red on the fifth floor, but stopped and waited for them when they saw Red was headed downstairs. Red smiled warmly. He purposely wanted the servants to feel comfortable being in his presence. He didn't want to alienate or intimidate them. He wanted to gain their confidence and trust, and he wanted them to come to him if they had questions or problems. "Is there an empty room on this floor where we can discuss the current situation concerning Don Castillo and this building?"

A matronly woman who appeared to be in her late forties pointed down the hall. "There's an apartment at the end of the hall that is set up as a sort of conference room. We can go there to talk if you'd like," she said.

"Lead the way," Red said.

The room proved to be as plush as the rooms on the top floor. "What's your name?" Red asked the woman.

"Annette," she said.

"I'm Red. How many employees are there working in the castle?"

"There are twenty-one employees that work here."

"Wow! That many, eh?"

"Don Castillo insists on twenty-four-hour service, so we work three shifts."

"I see. Well, tell me this. Does he treat you well?"

Annette gulped and looked at her fellow employees, pleading silently for help, but no help came, so she answered as best as she could. "Please, signore. I have to work for Don Castillo. Please don't make it difficult for us. We don't want Don Castillo to be angry with us. He can be a troublesome man when he is angry." Realizing that she may have said more than she should have, she apologized. "I'm sorry, I shouldn't talk about our employer to strangers."

"I'm not a stranger, Annette. I've taken control of the castle, and as for Don Castillo, he's no longer giving orders. I am. I'm in charge of this castle now, not Castillo. Understand?"

Annette looked at her fellow employees with an excited look on her face. "Are you serious, signore?"

"Yes. Very serious. I'll need help from some of you because I'm not sure of how or where Castillo made his money. I want to give all the current employees a ten percent raise in pay, but I want to make sure we can afford it."

"Signore Red. Be careful, because if Don Castillo returns

The Sicilian Caper

and if he didn't agree to have you run his castle, he can be a very dangerous person."

"Let me clarify something right now, Annette. Don Castillo is dead. He died tragically in an accident right here in this castle, so I wouldn't worry about him harassing you employees or bothering me. The man is dead... period. Now I'd like to know how he made his money, and I want one of you to tell me now."

A man raised his hand. "I'm Reggie the gardener, sir. I take care of the grounds around the castle. Don Castillo owns many other properties which he rents, and he collects rent money from those people."

"I see," Red said. "I don't like surprises. Are there any surprises waiting for me in this castle that I don't already know about?"

A man raised his hand. "I'm Eric and I take care of the automobiles."

"How many automobiles do you take care of, Eric?"

"We have six cars and a utility van that seats nine people. All six vehicles, although old, I'm proud to say are in pristine condition, including the van."

"Is there anything you could add to what I've already been told?"

"No, sir. There's nothing more I can add, except, of course, for the gambling equipment in the basement."

"Bingo!" Red said silently to himself while trying hard to stifle a smile. "Please show me the basement and the gambling equipment later, Eric."

"No problem, sir. When you're ready, you'll find me in the garage. I'm changing the plugs in the 1961 Ferrari 250 GT California Spider classic and tuning the little bugger up, so it keeps running like it should."

"I want to see the rest of the castle. It shouldn't take long, and then I'll stop by the garage. By the way, Eric, where is the garage?"

"The garage is behind the castle. In the old days, it used to be the stables, but when automobiles came into vogue, they changed the stables to house the automobiles. Of course, over the years, with the addition of multiple cars, we've had to expand the stables, so it would be difficult to miss them. But don't worry, sir, I'll send Henry to you, and he'll guide you to my shop. Henry is my assistant."

"Thank you, Eric, and I appreciate you sending Henry to me. It'll make it easier if he takes me to the garage." Eric turned to leave, but Red stopped him. "Have you been in the garage yet this morning, Eric?"

"No, sir. Why do you ask?"

"Just wondering. We heard a rumbling inside the walls of the castle this afternoon, and I thought maybe there might have been a collapse or possibly an earthquake. Just be careful when entering the garage, Eric."

"Thank you, sir. That's very thoughtful of you to be concerned for the hired help." Red hoped the garage was far enough away from the castle that it wouldn't have been affected by the internal collapse caused by the four traps being triggered. It would be a shame if the collapse set off by the traps damaged or destroyed any of those fine automobiles. He'd find out soon enough, though. The garage was the next stop after the castle for Red. He was eager to see the castle's basement, and he wanted a deeper understanding of just what transpired in the basement and what gambling equipment had to do with it. Was Castillo running an illegal gambling operation? Was the gambling by invitation only? Or was Castillo connected to the Sicilian mob, as partners maybe?

There was nothing unusual about the rest of the castle, nor the help's excited murmuring. They knew things were different now. At first, they had difficulty believing the old Don was no longer their boss, and they didn't believe he was dead. They feared Don Castillo. He was a ruthless dictator in dealing with the help, and the help feared him for his cruelty. Silently, they were happy to hear he had died, but they were worried that they were no longer needed and they'd lose their jobs. Red understood their concerns, and before he went down to the garage to see Eric, he assuaged their fears by explaining to them that not only wouldn't they be fired, but he intended to see that all the help received raises, which changed their attitudes from one of fear to one of anticipation, something they hadn't felt in a long time.

After visiting every room on every floor, Henry took Red

The Sicilian Caper

down to the garage, where Eric was waiting patiently to show him the automobiles they charged him with keeping in showroom condition and in perfect running order. "Ahh, Mr. Red. I'm thrilled to show you our collection of automobiles. The first is, of course, is the 1961 Ferrari 250 GT California Spider Classic I've just tuned up." The car was a classic red beauty. "And this, of course, is or was the master's car of choice. It is a 1937 V12 Rolls-Royce Phantom III, which was introduced in 1936. It is a wonderful, luxurious touring car, Mr. Red, and it is a most comfortable automobile to ride in. Like I said, this was Mr. Castillo's favorite car." Eric pulled a tarp off of a smaller car, which turned out to be a red 1957 two-door Ford Thunderbird, with a 312 CID V8 engine, air conditioning, power windows, power doors, and an automatic transmission. "I prefer the 1957 Thunderbird to the 1955 and '56 because of rust problems. As you can see, this car remains like new thanks to the care it has received over the intervening years. This car is a 1961 Jaguar XKE." He pulled a tarp off, revealing a red XKE. This was the first year of production for this car."

Red nodded and replied, "Another red car, Eric?"

"It is a sports car, Mr. Red. Are there any other colors for a sports car?"

Red laughed out loud. "Hell no, Eric. You're right, there are no other colors but red for a sports car. Now show me your next car."

Eric pulled the tarp off of the next to the last car and Red's eye's widened as a powder blue 1958 Edsel citation convertible emerged. The car was in new condition. "Have you ever driven this car?" Red asked.

"Very little, sir. It still has under one thousand original miles on the odometer."

"Blue? What happened to red?"

"Blue because it is a convertible and not a true sports car. That is why the color of the car is blue, sir."

"I see," Red said, stifling a smile.

Red spotted a car against the wall with a car cover over it. "What is under that cover, Eric?"

"That cover is hiding a real treat, sir. It hides the sixth car. A very special car worth over a million dollars."

"Really?" Red said.

"Come, I'll show you the car. It is a 1930 LeBaron Barrelside Duesenberg." Eric lifted the cover off of the classic automobile and the beautiful condition it was in took Red's breath away.

"My God, but this is a beautiful automobile."

"That it is, sir, and Mr. Castillo bought this car brand new. It only has twenty-four thousand miles on the odometer. Now that you have seen the cars, sir, would you like to see the gambling equipment I spoke to you earlier about?"

"I thought you'd never ask, Eric. Lead the way." When they left the garage, Red looked up at the towering castle's ominous ramparts. "Are you sure you didn't feel a tremor earlier Eric?"

"No, sir. I hadn't felt a thing."

"I see," Red said and remained silent as Eric led Red around the house, to a side entrance into the cellar. They walked down a short flight of stairs into a hallway past a maze of rooms. Eric stopped in front of one locked door, took out his key, and unlocked the door. He leaned over and clicked a switch on the wall that lit the entire room. It was a large room, filled with tables and games of chance, such as roulette wheels, blackjack tables, dice or craps tables and every sort of gambling apparatus imaginable lay there waiting to be assembled and placed into position in the room so hopeful suckers could legally be separated from their money.

Tarzan leaned over and whispered to Red. "What do ya think, Red?"

"I think we're going to have a casino in Sicily, that's what I think."

"But what, Red? I know that uncertainty in your voice. Something isn't sitting right with you."

"Very perceptive of you, Tarzan, and you're right. Before we go any further, I have to find out if Castillo and the Sicilian mob had a gambling interest, and if so, I have to find out what that interest is. If the Sicilian mob wasn't involved with Castillo, then we have to find out the legalities of opening a casino in Gratteri, and if we get that far with no interference from the local government or the local mob, then we have to find someone we trust to operate it for us."

The Sicilian Caper

"How are we going to do that, boss? We don't know many people in Sicily we can trust."

"First, we have to get past the legalities of opening a casino in Sicily. Then we can find someone to run it, and I have a few ideas we can kick around concerning that. But before we get ahead of ourselves, I have to take over ownership of the castle. Pissclam, get Captain Frankie and tell him I want to speak to him."

"Okay, boss. I'll be right back."

Fifteen minutes later, Pissclam led Captain Frankie into the castle's basement and to where Red waited, with Tarzan and Eric examining the gambling tables.

"You wanted to see me, Red?"

"Yes, Frankie. I'm sending you to Las Vegas to pick up Ernie. I need him here to help me with a few things." Frankie didn't question Red on what those things he needed help with were. It was none of his business and he couldn't talk about what he didn't know. He knew one thing, and that was Red did nothing without a good reason. So if he wanted Ernie here, he must have one helluva great reason for me to get him. The cost to fuel the jet to fly to and from America would bankrupt the average family, so Captain Frankie knew Red must have a powerful need for him to use the jet to get Ernie. "Tarzan... set up a transatlantic call to Las Vegas and when you get a line, call Ernie and tell him I'm sending a jet to get him. I need him here as soon as possible."

"Okay, Red. I'll call the international phone operator to set up the call now." A little while later, Tarzan returned. "We got lucky, Red. They set the call for tomorrow morning."

"Good. Now I can tell Captain Frankie to prepare to fly out of here tomorrow morning for Vegas." Then Red remembered he sent Pissclam to get Sophia. "Pissclam, did you get Sophia?"

"Yes boss, she's upstairs."

"Go get her and bring her down here."

"Okay, boss."

"Tarzan. You had two fabric envelopes earlier, and you only opened one of them. What about the second envelope? What was in that one?"

"Sorry about that, Red. I forgot to tell you I found the deed to the castle and the registrations for six cars and the van."

"Where's the envelope with the deed to the castle?"

"Upstairs, Red. I left it with the other envelope. It's in the room with the hidden door."

"Tell Pissclam where it is and then send him to get it. I don't want that deed out of our sight, not for a minute. Understand? That deed is our ticket to owning this castle and everything in it."

"How many hours flying time would it take to get from Las Vegas to Sicily, Frankie?"

"It's about 6,086 miles and flying at 500 hundred miles per hour. It would take 12 hours and 40 minutes of flying time. Sal is my co-pilot, so he'll have to fly back with me, and then figure on us laying over a day before we begin our return trip. I'll need a credit card to charge for refueling."

"I'd like you to leave first thing in the morning. Tarzan can handle the phone call to Ernie in Vegas. When he calls Ernie, I want you halfway there already. If you're tired and you feel you're not ready to fly back to Sicily, then spend an extra day, but as soon as you're ready, I want you in the air. Understand?"

"You wanted to see me, Red?"

It was Sophia, and she appeared at just the right moment. "How would you like to go to the United States with Captain Frankie, Sophia? It would only be for a day, maybe two days, and then you'll fly back. He's flying to Vegas to pick up one of my men that I need with me here. It's a twelve-hour trip both ways, and I would need you to act as an airline hostess to serve coffee and a meal. The meals are pre-made, but you'll have to make the coffee. If you decide to go, I'll pay you one hundred dollars a day, plus your meals and room and board."

Sophia was more excited to be flying to the fabulous Las Vegas she read so much about than anything else, other than the gold Rolex and her fur coat, that had happened to her in her young life. This was a pre-paid vacation/adventure that she looked forward to going on, and the best part was she was being paid handsomely just to pour coffee and serve a few pre-cooked meals to a few of Red's friends. She took note that ever since she tended to Joey Boys' wounds, her fortune had picked up considerably, and going on this trip was an unexpected bonus.

The Sicilian Caper

Red jarred her from her thoughts, when he called her name. "Yes, Red. Sorry, but my mind was on other things."

Red narrowed his eyes and looked at her closely. "Are you sure you want to take this job, Sophia?"

"Are you kidding me, Red? Right now, I think I'd shoot you if you were to tell me you changed your mind about sending me on this trip. I've never left Sicily, and this is my chance to visit Las Vegas, which I heard and read so much about."

Red reached into his pocket and pulled out a roll of bills and he peeled off three one-hundred-dollar bills. "Use these bills to play the casino, but don't get carried away, because gambling is a sucker's game. The house always wins in the long run. Remember that." He pulled Tarzan aside. "Watch her and make sure she wins a little money, but not enough for her to make a fool of herself. Understand?"

"I understand, Red. It should be an interesting trip for Sophia, and one that she'll talk about for years. I'll make sure she enjoys herself."

"Is Joey Boy strong enough to go with you, Frankie?"

"He's healing well, and the trip won't hurt him at all."

"Then take Joey Boy with you. He can be her escort and make sure she enjoys herself without getting herself in trouble. There are always the grifters looking to take something from someone that isn't theirs. See that Joey Boy knows not to let that happen to her."

"If Joey Boy is with her, he won't have to be told anything. I pity the guy that tries to pull a scam on Sophia with Joey Boy watching after her."

"Good. It's settled then."

Sophia turned to leave. She wanted to get ready for her flight tomorrow, but Red stopped her. "Sophia, I told you I would pay for your medical school. I need to know exactly how much money it would cost to finish your medical education."

Sophia knew the amount by heart. It was all she ever thought of before meeting Red and his men. "Twenty-five thousand dollars American money would pay for my education, Red."

"We'll talk more about this when you return to Sicily."

Red gave last-minute instructions to Frankie the Pilot, and

instead of sleeping at Sophia's home, Red had Eric take everyone to a hotel near the airport in the Rolls Royce. Everyone had their own room, including Sophia. They scheduled takeoff for 6:30 am. Red wanted the plane to arrive in Las Vegas early enough for Ernie to meet them upon landing at the airport twelve hours later. Just before getting into the Rolls, Red handed Frankie an attaché case. "When you get to the States, bring this attaché case to our bank in Vegas, and have the manager handle the payment for the jet. Tell him to overnight the cash to Fred Thompson at the Long Island Executive Airport in Islip to pay for the jet I bought from him, so make sure he over-nights you the title to the aircraft and a receipt that says paid in full."

"I'll make sure Thompson receives the money for the jet and that he sends me the title to the plane."

"Good. That's a load off of my mind. At least now I can relax knowing the plane is mine, and it's paid for. We'll have the Double Seven Casino take ownership of the plane. This way, we can write it off as a business investment. Have Ernie take care of that before you fly back to Sicily with him."

CHAPTER 20

The business jet touched down smoothly at McCarran International Airport and, as instructed by the air traffic controller, taxied to the proper hangar, where Ernie waited patiently for them to de-plane.

"Hi, Ernie."

"Hi, Captain Frankie, Joey Boy, Sal, Ron, and who is this pretty lady?" Ernie asked.

"Say hello to Sophia, Ernie." Joey Boy leaned in close to Ernie. "This pretty lady saved my life when they shot me full of holes, and I was leaking like a bucket with a lot of holes in it."

"Damn, Joey Boy, I never saw a guy who was shot so full of bullet holes, so many times that he could be mistaken for a big hunk of Swiss cheese. When we get back to the Double Seven, I want to hear all about it, without you leaving anything interesting out."

Joey Boy laughed. "It's a good thing Sophia is a medical student who knew what she was doing. She took the bullets out and sewed me up. She took good care of me, and if it wasn't for her, I wouldn't have pulled through." Ernie cast a sidelong glance at Sophia, and with it, came a newfound respect for the lady.

The lights along the main drag lit up the strip, making it seem to Sophia they were riding into a fairyland. "My God," Sophia gasped. "This is like riding into a dream. This place is wonderful."

Ernie shook his head. "Don't let the glitter fool you. This is the boulevard of broken dreams, honey, where only the strong survive."

Ernie took Tarzan aside. "What do we do with the broad?"

"Red wants her to have a good time. He wants her to win a little, just enough to make it memorable for her, but not enough to make her crazy. This trip was his reward to her for saving Joey Boys' life, which she definitely did. Look at Joey Boy fawning all over her. I think he's in love with her. He doesn't let her out of his sight. As long as she's in the States, he'll be her protector."

"She knows we'll be leaving soon, right?"

"She knows. I told her she has to get her sleep because she has to be alert enough to serve her passengers their food and drinks. But don't worry, I'll tell Joey Boy to monitor her and make sure he drags her to her hotel to get some sleep. She knows that we'll be leaving bright and early the day after tomorrow early in the morning, so it shouldn't be a problem."

"Do you know what Red wants with me in Sicily, Tarzan?"

"I have an idea what he wants from you, but I'd rather he told you."

"It must be important if he sent his brand new, just bought personal jet from Sicily all the way to America just to get me."

"It is important, Ernie, or he wouldn't have sent me to get you, but I would rather he told you what he wants from you, rather than you hearing it from me."

"When does Captain Frankie plan on leaving, Tarzan?"

"We're leaving the day after tomorrow very early in the morning. Red insisted that Captain Frankie needed a day of rest. Red wants us in Sicily as soon as possible. It's a twelve-hour flight, so if we leave at 6 am, we'll be there in twelve hours. Tomorrow will be a day of lounging by the pool," Tarzan advised.

"I'm going to say goodnight. I'd better head to my hotel and get a good night's sleep. See you guys tomorrow morning in the dining room."

"That's why we brought Sophia with us. Red hired her to make the coffee and served the meals. When we get on the plane, you won't have to rush to finish your breakfast, because you can eat your meals on the plane."

The crew lounged around the pool during the day and Joey Boy took Sophia to dinner and to a show she'd never forget. Elvis was in town and Joey Boy pulled some strings and got

The Sicilian Caper

tickets to his show. They were up early the following day and had breakfast on the plane.

Eric waited at the airport for the business jet to land. He brought the Rolls Royce to pick up Red's men and Sophia. Henry followed Eric in the van in case more passenger room was needed.

Gratteri Castle - Following Day

"What did you want to see me about, Red? I know it must be important because you bought a plane and used it to bring me here from America. Now why did you bring me here and what can I do for you?"

Red poured Ernie, Tarzan, and himself another cup of the strong Italian coffee. Ernie laughed. "That bad, eh?"
"I have had none of the rooms in the castle swept for bugs, so I'm always a little nervous talking shop without checking for bugs first. I'm going to talk low, so lean closer to me because what I have to say is for our ears only. Hand me the deed to the castle, Tarzan. I want this deed signed over to me. I have witnesses that will sign an affidavit that I bought the castle from Don Castillo for a pre-determined amount, who after being paid, Castillo then signed the castle and everything in it over to me, and that includes the cars."

"I need a sample of Castillo's handwriting and the deed to the castle." Tarzan supplied both items to Ernie, who studied Castillo's handwriting before practicing on a blank sheet of paper.

"That's almost perfect, Ernie. I can't tell the difference between Castillo's handwriting and yours."

"The signature is close, but not perfect. Give me a few more minutes to practice his writing, and I'll nail it," Ernie said with assured confidence.

"As soon as you can write Castillo's name exactly the same as Castillo, you'll sign the deed to the castle over to me, and then we'll head to Mario's tobacco shop, and I'll ask him how to register the sale of the castle over to me. I have a few questions concerning the local mafia I have to ask Mario, and I'm hoping he'll be able to answer them for me," Red told Ernie.

"Come on. I'm done here. Let's go to see Mario and get answers to your questions."

Red and Ernie waited for Mario to finish taking care of a customer. "Hello, Red. What brings you into my store?"

"I came in here to let you know I bought the old castle from Castillo. He's no longer in the picture, and he won't be bothering anyone any longer."

"Do you mean he won't be bothering anyone permanently?"

"That's exactly what I mean. He's no longer among the living, and that's one reason I have to talk to you. I discovered enough gambling equipment in the castle's cellar to open a casino. I thought maybe you can help me understand the gambling laws in Sicily, and I was hoping you could tell me where I could find the local mafiosi. I wouldn't want to open up a gambling casino in the castle without an understanding between me and the people who control the rackets in this part of Sicily."

"Ask Muro to take you to his uncle Aldo Muro. He's the power behind the rackets in this part of Sicily. Get his approval to open a casino and you'll have no problems with the law, as Aldo Muro controls the law in this region of Sicily. Don't be surprised if he asks for a percentage of the profits. It would be worth it to you to give him ten percent of the profits for his protection from the law. As a minority partner, he'll protect you from other more unsavory competitors."

"Pissclam."

"Yes, boss?"

"Do you know where Muro is?"

"Yes, boss, he's waiting by the car with some men."

"Go get him. Tell him I want to see him right away. It's important."

When Red explained what he wanted Muro to do, Muro's eyes widened like the headlights on the Rolls. "I can't do that, Red. My uncle would kill me if I showed up at his place, asking for a favor. He sent me to protect Don Castillo, and instead, I double-crossed Castillo."

"Why did your uncle agree to protect Castillo? Was he a

The Sicilian Caper

friend of his?"

"No. My uncle didn't like Castillo, and he had little respect for him, but he was the Don of Gratteri, and my uncle respected his position even though he didn't respect him."

"Set up a meeting between me and your uncle, and I promise you, the meeting will be a success."

"He'll kill me, Red. I know he will."

"No one will kill anyone, not while I'm there. Trust me when I tell you no one will be killed while I'm meeting with your uncle Aldo Muro, and that includes you, Muro. Besides, he probably doesn't know that Castillo is dead yet, and if that's the case, it can be used to our advantage. Besides, I never had a meeting that I couldn't control, and one way or another, I always control the meeting. Call your uncle and make the appointment. Tell him Big Red Fortunato from Queens, New York is in Sicily and would like a few minutes of his time. Tell him it could be profitable for both of us."

Red could tell the last thing Giuseppi Muro wanted to do was to ask his uncle to meet with Red. It was the part of his conversation when he told his uncle that Red said it may be profitable for both men to have this meeting. It was curiosity that prompted Muro to agree to meet with Red tomorrow at noon at his headquarters, which was nothing more than a social club that served drinks and coffee, and Red opted for coffee, which he knew would be fresh, rich and enjoyable.

Giuseppi led Red, Tarzan, Trenchie, and Pissclam into Aldo Muro's club, where two men patted them down for weapons. "They're clean," one man told Muro in Italian, which Tarzan understood and passed what they said to Red, but Red understood some of the Sicilian dialect and had understood what the man told Muro.

"Tarzan, tell Muro that we came to this meeting as friends and we intend to leave as friends."

Tarzan told Muro what Red said, and that Tarzan spoke Sicilian both surprised and pleased Muro. "Please sit down and we'll enjoy a cup of espresso, or a drink, if you prefer," Aldo Muro offered.

"Coffee would be great, thank you." Muro smiled and snapped his fingers and men jumped at his command. Soon, they set a pot of coffee and a plate of pastry in front of Red and his men.

Muro turned to his nephew. "You had better have a good excuse for disobeying me and not guarding Castillo."

Red understood enough of what Muro told his nephew. He raised a hand to interject his thoughts into the conversation. "Tarzan, explain to Mr. Muro that Castillo sold his castle to me, and that is why I asked for this meeting. I don't want any misunderstanding between us."

Tarzan told Muro what Red said, and the look on Muro's face said it all. "Where is Castillo now?" Muro asked.

"Tell Mr. Muro that he's dead, and if he asks how he died, tell him exactly what I tell you to tell him."

"He asked me how he died, Red. What do you want me to tell him?"

"Tell him he tried to kill me but failed. He killed one of my men and wounded another seriously. To save his life, he agreed to sell me his castle. After signing the deed over to me, he tried to escape through a hidden door, but he triggered one of the four traps and it killed him."

Muro shook his head. "That sounds like something that pig would do... make a deal and then renege on it. I want to hear Red tell me his story from the beginning."

Red, through Tarzan, told Aldo Muro the entire story right from beginning. "And the fool thought to escape, and when he thought when he was alone and no one was looking, he bolted through the hidden door to his doom. There was nothing behind that door after that section of the mountain collapsed into nothingness."

Muro nodded, but the old mafioso knew something more made Castillo disappear. "Very convenient. Castillo disappearing soon after he sells you his castle. But that aside, you still haven't told me how we would make money."

"I found a lot of gambling equipment in the basement of the old castle, and I could always recognize an opportunity to make money when I saw it. I want to open a legal gambling casino in the basement of the old castle. The basement is plenty large enough to accommodate a large group of gamblers, and with a little help, I know the Sicilian authorities would grant us a

The Sicilian Caper

gambling license."

Muro nodded. "I just heard the word 'us' bandied about, along with the authorities granting us a gambling license. How does the 'us' concern me?"

Red lit a cigar and pointed it at Aldo Muro. "I could use someone with clout in this region of Sicily to handle the law and competitors."

Muro rubbed his chin, contemplating what Red just told him. "And what exactly would this someone get for his troubles?"

"He would get ten percent of the all profits from gambling."

"I see," Muro said. "I like the sound of that, but I'd like the sound of twenty percent of the profits better."

Red shook his head. "I can't do that, Muro, but I'll tell you what. I feel generous today, so we'll split the difference. I'll agree to give you fifteen percent of all the profits we receive from gambling. Every month, a full accounting will be given to you detailing how much money we made from gambling, and how much of that was profit. I would imagine your share of the profits would be in the millions of dollars."

Red caught Muro's reaction as his eyes widened at the mention of millions of dollars in profit going into Muro's coffers. "Who will run this operation?" Aldo Muro asked.

"I haven't decided yet, but the person I put in charge will be one of my men." Red noticed the suspicious look on Muro's face. "Relax, Muro. I never cheated a partner before, and I won't start now. Besides, you'll be free to examine the books whenever you want. If the man I choose ever cheated you or me, he'd be a dead man, and he'll know that, so relax and put your mind at ease. If we're going to have a partnership, there must be trust between us. You are the one who will be here, while I will be far away across the sea in America. Now do we have a deal, or will you force me to go around you, which I really don't want the hassle of doing. Now tell me. Is getting a gambling license going to be a problem?"

"No. I have contacts that will make getting a license a lot easier than usual."

"What concerns me as much as obtaining a gambling license is keeping the competition from becoming a nuisance. I don't want trouble from any would be wise guys, unions, and competitors. Can you handle problems I just mentioned that may occur in that area?"

Muro smiled and he ran his hand across his throat. "No. I can promise you that no one will bother us. In this region of Sicily, I am feared. Machiavelli stated in his book, *The Prince*, that it is better to be feared than loved." Muro shrugged. "I am not loved, Red, but I am feared."

"Look, Aldo. I just bought a new executive jet and I intend to send it here to bring some of my friends to America for a special night of food and entertainment at my club, the Starlight Club. I would like you to come as my guest."

"Can I bring my wife?"

"Of course, but I forgot to mention something that may change your mind about coming. One of my guests is Captain John Scatore. If that is a problem, I could have you travel by the airline of your choice. Of course, I'll have a word with Captain Scatore, and I'll let him know there is to be no business discussed on my private jet. I want everyone to be at ease, and enjoy the food and entertainment when on my plane or in my club."

"You mentioned the Starlight Club. Is that your club?" Muro asked Red.

"Yes, it is. You may have seen it in a movie. One of my men, James Roman, became a major movie star, and the Starlight Club was featured in his movie. In the United States, you will be perfectly safe, so there is no need to worry, but if there is room, you are welcome to take a bodyguard with you. When I get my passenger list, I'll let you know if that is a possibility."

"Wow! This partnership is getting off to a hell of a start, isn't it?" Muro said with a broad smile on his face.

"If you don't mind me asking, Red. Just what exactly is a captain in the Italian police department doing on your plane, and why is he going to America?"

Red smiled. "He's coming to New York at my invitation and he's taking his wife too, just like you're doing. That police officer is honest, and he can't be corrupted, but he did me a favor once, and I haven't forgotten. This trip is a sort of payback

The Sicilian Caper

from me, for that favor. We're still a long way off 'til that date, but I will keep you informed."

"Hmm, I see." Muro said, recognizing Red as a man of honor, and garnering a greater respect for him.

Red put out his hand and Muro took it. "It's a pleasure doing business with you, Aldo, and I feel a lot better knowing that you'll be watching over our gambling operation. I'll introduce you to the man or men who will represent me in this enterprise. I would do it now, but I haven't decided who I want to place in charge of the operation, but as soon as I do, I'll introduce you to him."

"Wait a minute, Red," Muro said, handing Red a slip of paper. "This is my private telephone number, and the second number is my beeper number. If I don't answer my private number, call my beeper number and I'll get back to you as soon as I can." What was surprising about talking to Muro was his English improved the longer they talked. Muro spoke English better than he let on, and that was his little secret. Sometimes it's better to play dumb than to educate your opponent. Until now, Red had been his opponent, but now that they were partners in a gambling enterprise, he allowed Red to know that he spoke better English than he led on or what Red had expected. There was no need for Tarzan to translate what Red said to Muro, because the man understood every word Red said to Tarzan, but he kept that little secret to himself. Red respected Muro for keeping the fact that he understood English, because that was something he would have done had he understood and spoken the Sicilian dialect well. It was a way to learn something unexpected, and useful from a man you didn't know well enough to trust yet.

The smooth transfer of the castle from Castillo to Red was routine, especially with Aldo Muro's help. Ernie remained in Sicily, albeit reluctantly, to help convert the castle's medieval cellar, which still contained the complete trappings of torture, including an iron maiden, into an inviting, modern gambling casino and restaurant, with just enough of the old castle's macabre ambiance to make interesting conversation over dinner, where a portion of the first floor's large ballroom was remodeled into a sumptuous dining area and set aside for

171

members only. Red liked the idea of owning a castle in Sicily. Sometimes in his career when the law forced him to disappear for a while, and it was always difficult to find a place where he'd be safe from the law. In Sicily, he'd have such a place, especially having a powerful friend in Sicily, such as Aldo Muro.

"Red, I'm not happy about this."

"I know, Ernie, I know. But look at it this way. It'll only be temporary, and to sweeten the deal, I'll cut you in for ten percent of the profits as long as you're here. As soon as you have everything set up properly and the casino making money, I'll send someone here to relieve you. You'll have to break him or her in first, but when you leave, you lose the ten percent. Agreed?"

Ernie's eyes widened. "Agreed, but did I hear you say "HER?"

"I was thinking of Sophia. She's smart as a whip and everyone in Gratteri knows her, and besides, she'll have Joey Boy watching over things here."

"Joey Boy?" Ernie asked, surprised at hearing Joey's name mentioned.

"Yeah, Joey Boy. The guy's in love with the gal. Ever since she saved his life, he's smitten with her, and I think if I told him he'd play a large part in keeping the castle a legitimate growing enterprise and part of his job would be to keep a close watch on Sophia. I think Joey Boy would jump at the chance, especially when I tell him about the title he'll have, and the pay raise I'll give him. Before we leave Sicily, I'll have a talk with Joey Boy, and we'll see if he accepts my offer, and between you and me, he'd be crazy to turn it down."

Ernie gave Red a tight-lipped smile. "I think the broad will clinch the deal, Red."

"Yeah, I agree. Now let's go have a talk with Sophia, and we'll see if we can sell her on the idea of managing the dining room."

CHAPTER 21

"I don't know what to say, Red. It's a wonderful opportunity, but I don't see how I'm qualified to run a gambling casino and restaurant. I have managed nothing, let alone a casino, so why me? And besides, I intend to go back to medical school. Why don't you hire someone with more experience?"

Red motioned to Tarzan. "Do we have any more of the bearer bonds here? Or did we send them all to America?"

"I kept two bundles here in case we needed them."

"Do we have $25,000 worth of the bearer bonds here?"

"I'm pretty sure we do, boss. Why?"

"It's paying for Sophia's medical schooling. And it's going to be like her working her way through college, only now she'll be in charge of the best dining room in this region of Sicily. You see, Sophia, experience isn't what I'm looking for. I need someone I trust who is familiar with this castle and the people in Gratteri. You'll have Joey Boy watching your back, and Aldo Muro's political connections, and If I find someone to relieve you of your position, I'll make it happen. Meanwhile, in your spare time, you'll have enough money to finish medical school."

"Do you have someone in mind to replace me, Red?" she asked hopefully.

"Yes, as a matter of fact I do, but I'm not sure he's interested in the job, but I intend to make him an offer he can't refuse. I'll know for sure before I leave for the States. If he accepts the job, then you have the money and you can go to college full time to finish your medical education." He patted her on her shoulder. "Don't worry, Sophia, I'll find someone to replace you. You'll only have to manage the dining room for a short while."

"How can I refuse you after giving me enough money to pay for my schooling?"

"Forget about it, Sophia. Me and the boys wanted to help you, and by giving you the money you need, it's our way of thanking you for the help you gave us. Now if you'll excuse me, I have to discuss business with Tarzan."

Red motioned for Tarzan to follow him to the office. "Close the door and make sure no one interrupts us, Tarzan." Red watched as Tarzan closed the door and then locked it. Red picked up the phone and dialed a number, and then he hung up.

A few minutes later, the beeper number he called returned his call. "This is Captain Scatore. Someone called my beeper number."

"John, it's Red. I need to see you as soon as your schedule permits."

"Are you in trouble, Red?"

"No. Just the opposite. I bought the Gratteri castle, and I'm converting the basement into a gambling casino. I'm also building a restaurant on the first floor. Renovations are taking place as we speak, and that's what I want to talk to you about. But not over the phone. I'd like to talk to you in private. So when can you get here?"

"Red, you continue to surprise me. I guess that's the charm of knowing you. I'll have a police helicopter fly me to the Palermo airport later this afternoon."

"Call me with the information and I'll have a car pick you up at the airport."

It surprised Captain Scatore to step into a Rolls Royce automobile in pristine condition, which made the drive to Gratteri smooth and special. When they arrived at the castle, they led Captain Scatore upstairs to the sumptuous room Red encountered when he first entered the room through the secret door. "John. How nice to see you again," Red said as Pissclam led Captain Scatore into the large, opulent room.

"It's a pleasure to see you again too, Red." Scatore's practiced eye scanned the faces of the strangers in the room with Red, and he immediately recognized Aldo Muro, which Red couldn't help noticing. All police officers in every country sometimes must not only deal with criminals, but they have to use them to their advantage. And most times, a friendship born of necessity is formed, and Captain John Scatore was no exception to the rule, and he exhibited that with a smile and a handshake upon being introduced to Aldo Muro. "It's nice to meet you too, Mr. Muro."

"And Red told me a lot about you too, Captain."

"I told Tarzan to bring you up here for a reason, John. I know being a police officer, you must have questions concerning the disappearance of Don Castillo and whether your American friend took ownership of this castle legally. I'd like to get those questions out of the way before I tell you the reason I asked you to come here.

"Come over here, John, and you too Aldo. I'm going to show you how Castillo died." The two men looked at one another, confusion written on their faces, but they both approached Red. "There was a secret door built into this wall hundreds of years ago. After Castillo sold me his castle, he must have thought we were going to kill him, which was far from the truth. I got what I wanted from him, and there was no need to resort to violence. I left him in Pissclam's care when I left the room. I'll let Pissclam tell you what happened after I left the room."

Pissclam was uncomfortable talking to a cop… any cop, and he looked at Red. "Do I have to do this, Red?"

"Yes. Just tell it like it happened, Pissclam."

Pissclam nodded and told his story. "As soon as Red left the room, Castillo waited for a chance to escape. When I left the room for a moment, he and his bodyguard bolted for the secret door and triggered the opening."

"Secret door?" Scatore asked.

"Yeah, the opening is right here.. Come over here and I'll show it to you." Both Captain Scatore and Aldo Muro followed Pissclam to a section of the wall. "You can't see it, but there's a door cleverly built into the wall."

"But I see nothing," Scatore said. Then Pissclam pushed the hidden lever, and the secret door clicked open. Both men looked out of the door into nothingness.

"Castillo stepped onto the stone that triggered the fourth trap, causing the floor under him to collapse into a large hollow in the mountain, and the falling boulders from the roof of the mountain killed him and his bodyguard instantly. Red didn't kill Castillo and his bodyguard, and neither did anyone else... the mountain killed them."

"Thanks, Pissclam." Red said, meaning it. "I just wanted to clear the record of how Castillo died. If we searched through the tons of rubble that fell on top of him, in about a month or two you might find what's left of Castillo... or maybe not. But either way, that's how he died."

Scatore removed his hanky and wiped his brow. "Thanks for clearing his death up for me, Red. To tell you the truth, my superiors had been questioning me about what I knew of Don Castillo's disappearance. This information you just told me justifies the use of a police helicopter, and now that we know how he died, we can close the investigation into Castillo's disappearance."

Red surprised Scatore by changing the subject. "When are you due to retire, John?"

"I have my time in, so I can retire whenever I decide to. Why do you ask?"

"Just so there is no misunderstanding between us, Aldo Muro is a minority partner in this enterprise. We both need someone honest, someone we can trust to manage the day-to-day operations of the casino and restaurant, and we were hoping you would accept the job. If you accept, you will receive a percentage of the profits, along with a staggering salary. I know how much you make as a captain of police, because you once told me. If you accept this position, you will make two or three times what you made as a police officer, plus a percentage of the profits I mentioned earlier. If you wish to have your wife near you, a suite of rooms in the castle will be available for you and your family at no cost to you, and we would include your meals. Understand this, John. Everything will be one hundred percent legitimate, and you will be in charge of making sure it stays that way."

"Wow. That is a wonderful offer, Red."

"That's right, and if you accept, you'll still receive your police department pension, plus what you make here. You and your family will live like potentates."

The Sicilian Caper

"I'll have to talk to my wife about this, Red. I'll need a couple of days before I can give you an answer."

"That's fine with me, John. How about you, Aldo? Do you have questions for the captain?"

"I have no questions but one. Do you mind working with someone who might be rumored as being on the other side of the law."

Scatore burst out laughing. "Might be rumored to be on the other side of the law? Please, Aldo... I have a file two inches thick on your activities, but in answer to your question, no, I don't mind working with someone like you, because I got to know you during the short time we met, even though you have in the past worked outside the law."

"You know, Red. I think I'm going to enjoy working with this cop." Muro said, meaning it.

Red took Ernie aside. "If Captain Scatore accepts the position to run this club, then you can come home with us. I'll have Sophia share the responsibility of running the place with Captain Scatore, until she leaves for medical school. When Sophia is gone, I'd like Scatore to run the restaurant, and the gambling operation. Before we leave, which should be one day this week, I'm expecting an answer from Scatore to let me know if he accepts the position, which he'd be a fool not to, and John Scatore is no fool. If he accepts my offer, I'll have a talk with him and Sophia, and I'll tell them what their duties are, and what I expect from them."

The Starlight Club: Two months later

Red was waiting by the Starlight Club's front window for Tarzan to return from Islip International Airport with his guests. He had sent Captain Frankie and Sal as his co-pilot to Palermo Airport to pick up his guests. Red told Muro to close the castle for the week he and Sophia would be on vacation, and he asked Aldo Muro to post a few of his men as castle guards, to make sure no one broke in the castle and caused mischief through robbery or vandalism. Muro was happy to oblige, which made Red rest easier. Joey Boy acted as maître d' and escorted Sophia, and Captain Scatore and his wife into the Starlight

Club, as well as two special guests that Red hadn't forgotten. Pissclam returned to the car and helped Mario and the frail old mafioso Dominick out of the car and stayed with them until they seated them at the table in the rear bar. In fact, Red gave Pissclam the responsibility of escorting all of Red's guests into the rear bar, where Red had a table set up for them. Even Giuseppi Muro and Tomasso were asked to nurse a drink at the rear bar.

Sophia sat next to a beautiful woman in a striking emerald evening gown. There were three young men sitting next to her and they looked vaguely familiar, but she couldn't quite figure out why. One man was a huge, well-built man, the other was a good-looking Latin man, but the quiet man with them was very good-looking in a rough sort of way. Sophia relaxed and fell into a comfortable conversation with Iris, and the two women who were about the same age took to one another. For Iris, it was good to be in the company of another woman her age, and so it was for Sophia too.

Red, who asked, "Is anyone ready for dinner?" interrupted them in their conversation. He waited for nods from everyone at the table, and when he got it, he waved his arm, and Tarzan pushed the button that opened the accordion doors into the dining room. The room lit up and Sophia gasped. She hadn't expected such beauty. Tarzan and Pissclam escorted Red's guests to a special table in front of the bandstand. The servers served champagne, and then they served the food, and the meal was as good as Red said it would be. After dinner, Red walked onto the bandstand and took the microphone. He thanked everyone for coming, and he warned them that the night was still young and he had special entertainment for them yet to come. "I also would like to introduce three young men who are not only world champion fighters in their respective weight class, but they have become three of the hottest young movie stars on the planet." Red introduced each of the fighters, which embarrassed Sophia because she sat and chatted with them without ever knowing they were movie stars. But it was when Red introduced Iris Lange that the room burst into applause. Iris Lange was the most famous female movie star in the world, and Sophia felt like a jerk, talking to her like she was just another

The Sicilian Caper

girl. Iris noticed the expression on Sophia's face, and she placed her hand on Sophia's. "Relax, Sophia. I may be a movie star to the public, but tonight, I'm just a girl having a wonderful conversation with another girl, and I might add, an exquisite-looking girl."

Red's voice stopped the conversations at each table. "Most of you know, a few times a year, I have a special Saturday night with special unannounced entertainment. Well, this is one of those exceptional Saturday nights. I promised you a fun night, and with our high-octane extra-special entertainers, you can't help but have a fun night, so for your entertainment, please welcome Louie Prima, and Keely Smith, with the Louie Prima band straight from the Flamingo Lounge in Las Vegas…"

The packed house loved Louie Prima and the stone-faced high energy Keely Smith. The energy the couple generated could have lit the Empire State building. They were at their best and the audience loved them.

The following day was a day of relaxation, where Red and his guests enjoyed good food and wonderful companionship. In the early afternoon, Pissclam parked Red's limousine in the parking lot across the street and waited for Red to instruct him what he wanted him to do. "Listen up, everyone. I'm taking Captain Scatore and his wife to the Aquacade for an afternoon of swimming in the sun. Tonight, I'll take them back to the Aquacade, where they will witness an entertaining, fun show they will talk about for years to come, and if you are interested, in the evening, we will visit the Copacabana nightclub for a night of good food and grand entertainment. Not as good as ours, of course, but good enough. Now, who wants to go with me?"

EPILOGUE

Present - Darien, Connecticut

"Well, Lynn, that's the story of how Red gained his castle in Gratteri, Sicily. The two Sicilian mobsters he took back to Queens with him worked out well for him. They missed their home in Sicily, but they loved the excitement of living in America. Joey Boy went back to Sicily as Red's eyes and ears, and besides, Joey fell in love with Sophia. I don't know if it was because she saved his life by pulling the bullets out of his back and then nursing him back to health, or if it was just love at first sight, but Joey Boy wouldn't let Sophia out of his sight. He wanted to be with her as much as possible. The free fur coats Sophia gave the women in Gratteri for Christmas were a tremendous surprise to the women, and the fur coats were a prize they could never afford on the salaries their husbands made. They could never afford those coats if they had to buy them with money they didn't have."

"Did Iris keep in touch with Sophia?" Lynn asked her father.

"I don't know, Lynn. Although I imagine Iris was a pretty busy lady back then. That's a question I'll try to find the answer to."

"Thanks, Dad. This story differed from all the other stories you told me about the Starlight Club. I mean, it mostly took place in a little town in Sicily, and it concerned an old castle built high on a mountain top."

"They built all castles on the top of a mountain, Lynn. By doing that, they could see if the enemy marching toward them was a threat, and having the high ground, the defenders in the castle could better protect themselves."

The Sicilian Caper

AUTHOR'S NOTES

While the story is fictitious, some of the characters were real as well as some instances in the story.

1 Jeannie-Leg-and-a-half was a very attractive young lady who had polio as a child. Her illness left her with a shriveled leg, which caused her to walk with a noticeable limp. She was a very attractive young lady with natural blond hair, blue eyes, and a fair complexion, as well as a nice figure. She was respected by both men and women because of the way she comported herself, but she wasn't psychic. I gave her that ability to enhance the story line.

2 Ernie's land in Argentina was real. It was owned by Doctor Texacas, a brilliant man who owned many patents in different categories, such as automobiles, industrial, home, and so on. His family owned the property mentioned in the book. He trusted Ernie and had him represent him. Ernie told me his art work still hangs in Mexico City. During the second World War, the doctor's property's easy access should have been selected for use by the US government, but as usual, politics entered into the equation, and a property difficult to get to and extremely expensive to extract the rubber needed for our war effort was governed by politics.

3 Tarzan and Ernie's trial in Mineola, Long Island was real and Jimmy Hoffa did send Bennet Williams, his attorney, to represent them. Hoffa paid for the trial and Bennet's time.

4 Ernie did in fact work for Jimmy Hines, the power behind the

Governor of New York.

5 Ralph was a real person and as dangerous in real life as he was in the book.

The Sicilian Caper

Also by Joe Corso

The Comeback
The Time Portal
Lafitte's Treasure
Gunfight in Abilene
Shootout in Cheyenne
The Last Gun-Shark
the Lone Jack Kid series
The Revenge of John W
The Time Traveler series
The Starlight Club series
The Old Man and the King
Engine 24 Fire Stories series
Tommy Topper and the Pixie Princess

www.corsobooks.com
954-295-2765

Thank you for reading my book. I hope you enjoyed reading it as much as I enjoyed writing it. Reviews are very important to an author. So if you liked this story, this author would appreciate it if you left a review on Amazon telling of your experience.

Made in the USA
Columbia, SC
14 March 2024